Ther__ _____ _____ ___ __ un-
derbrus_____ _____ ___ __ stepped out onto
the road. Under his battered brown Indiana Jones hat his hair was thick and sort
of butterscotch colored. He had on jeans, a
T-shirt with CAMP CHEROKEE across the front,
and scuffed leather hiking boots. As far as
I was concerned, he looked just about
perfect.

He gave me an appraising glance. "You
must be Tabitha, right? I can tell you're
from the city."

"I'm from Washington," I said. "I'm going
to be a counselor at Cherokee."

The boy looked at me. "You know, I don't
understand why Pete had to go all the way
to the city to hire a counselor. You'd think
he'd find somebody who knows her way
around the woods."

"I've been to camp," I said defensively. "I
went to Girl Scout day camp two years ago.
They taught us how to paddle a canoe and
build fires and tie knots."

"Well then," he said with a grin, "I guess
we'll make you responsible for tying all the
knots in camp."

Bantam Sweet Dreams Romances
Ask your bookseller for the books you have missed

#1   P.S. I LOVE YOU
#18 TEN-BOY SUMMER
#20 THE POPULARITY SUMMER
#63 KISS ME, CREEP
#77 TEN-SPEED SUMMER
#89 101 WAYS TO MEET
     MR. RIGHT
#92 KISS AND TELL
#93 THE GREAT BOY CHASE
#96 FIRST, LAST, AND ALWAYS
#105 THE PERFECT BOY
#117 THE OTHER ME
#118 HEART TO HEART
#120 MR. WONDERFUL
#121 ONLY MAKE-BELIEVE
#122 STARS IN HER EYES
#123 LOVE IN THE WINGS
#124 MORE THAN FRIENDS
#125 PARADE OF HEARTS
#126 HERE'S MY HEART
#127 MY BEST ENEMY
#128 ONE BOY AT A TIME
#129 A VOTE FOR LOVE

#130 DANCE WITH ME
#131 HAND-ME-DOWN HEART
#132 WINNER TAKES ALL
#133 PLAYING THE FIELD
#134 PAST PERFECT
#135 GEARED FOR ROMANCE
#136 STAND BY FOR LOVE
#137 ROCKY ROMANCE
#138 HEART AND SOUL
#139 THE RIGHT COMBINATION
#140 LOVE DETOUR
#141 WINTER DREAMS
#142 LIFEGUARD SUMMER
#143 CRAZY FOR YOU
#144 PRICELESS LOVE
#145 THIS TIME FOR REAL
#146 GIFTS FROM THE HEART
#147 TRUST IN LOVE
#148 RIDDLES OF LOVE
#149 PRACTICE MAKES PERFECT
#150 SUMMER SECRETS
#151 FORTUNES OF LOVE

Sweet Dreams Specials

A CHANGE OF HEART
MY SECRET LOVE
SEARCHING FOR LOVE
TAKING THE LEAD
NEVER SAY GOODBYE
A CHANCE TO LOVE

Summer Secrets

Susan Blake

BANTAM BOOKS
TORONTO • NEW YORK • LONDON • SYDNEY • AUCKLAND

RL 6, IL age 11 and up

SUMMER SECRETS
A Bantam Book / August 1988

ISBN 0-553-27357-4

Published simultaneously in the United States and Canada

PRINTED IN THE UNITED STATES OF AMERICA

O   0 9 8 7 6 5 4 3 2 1

Summer Secrets

Chapter One

"How many days to go?" Megan wanted to know. It was the third time she'd asked that morning.

"Only six more," I said patiently, pointing to the calendar on my desk. The day we were leaving together for Camp Sail-Away was circled in red.

Megan sighed. "Six whole days? I'll never make it!"

I pulled a green and white cotton top from the heap of clothes on my bed and held it up. "So what do you think about this? I could wear it with my white jeans, or over my new bathing suit." I hadn't shown the bathing suit to my mother yet. She's kind of old-fashioned about how much of me should actually be seen on the beach.

Megan considered for a minute. "Yeah, that top would be good. I could wear it with my black shorts. I mean, what's the point of our going away together, Tabby, if we don't share our clothes?" She plopped down on the carpet and sighed dreamily. "Isn't it *super*? Three whole weeks at Sail-Away!"

I sat on the bed and pulled my knees up to my chin. "I know," I said. "I'm still pinching myself. Especially after Dad's check came and everything was made definite."

Sail-Away, a super-sophisticated sailing camp on Chesapeake Bay, wasn't exactly cheap. My mother and father are divorced, and I knew that if I'd had to ask Mother for camp tuition, I could forget about going. She makes a pretty good salary working in one of the congressional offices, but it costs a fortune to live in Washington, D.C. So when Megan came up with the idea of our going to Sail-Away together, I'd asked my dad for an advance present for my sixteenth birthday, which was four months away. He'd sent the check and a nice letter telling me to have a good time. I was already planning to have a *terrific* time.

"The best part," Megan said, lying on her

back to do her bike-pedaling exercise, "is that the boys outnumber the girls at this place. I've got to lose at least five pounds before we go," she puffed, pedaling furiously. "Do you think I can?"

"*No* problem," I answered with a grin, glancing pointedly at the empty ice-cream bowls on the floor. We'd just eaten two big scoops of strawberry. "We *both* can—if we totally give up eating for the next six days."

Megan dropped her legs with a thump. "*You* don't need to lose five pounds, Tabby," she said. "You're fine just the way you are."

I stood up and glanced in the mirror again. I'd always liked the dark hair and turned-up nose I'd inherited from my mother, and my father's green eyes were perfectly acceptable. And even if I'd been inclined to gain weight, I probably *couldn't* have, living with my mother. She's just fine in most ways, but when it comes to eating, she's a health-food maniac. I figured it would be impossible to get fat munching alfalfa sprouts and brown rice for dinner. Even our strawberry "ice-cream" was really made out of yogurt.

Out in the hall, the phone rang. I've been lobbying for a phone in my bedroom, but Mother says it would cost an arm and a leg.

3

I'd settle for an extension cord under the door, I told her. She said she'd take it under consideration.

I opened the door and reached for the phone, but Mother had gotten to it first. I listened for a second to make sure that the call wasn't for me. It wasn't.

"Oh, *Pete!*" my mother was saying happily. She leaned against the wall and gave me a signal with her eyebrows that meant to go away. "I'm so glad to hear from you! How are you and Joan making out with the new business?"

"It's only Uncle Pete," I told Megan, coming back into the bedroom and closing the door. Uncle Pete was my mother's favorite brother.

"Isn't he the one who just bought the summer camp for kids?" Megan asked, scouting around for her tennis shoes. I fished one out from under a purple sweatshirt and handed it to her.

"Yeah," I said. "In the middle of the Blue Ridge Mountains." I shuddered. "With bears and wolves and snakes!"

Uncle Pete and Aunt Joan have always been my favorite relatives because they go on interesting adventures—and then come home and show slides that *don't* bore you to death.

4

They've climbed mountains in Alaska and visited monasteries in Nepal. But this spring they had done what I considered to be a *very* weird thing—they had left perfectly good jobs in New York to run a rough-it camp in the woods for kids, complete with bunkhouses and outdoor toilets. I guess something like that might sound interesting to other people, but not to me. You get used to the good life living in Washington. My idea of the perfect camp is Sail-Away, which has a heated swimming pool and two saunas and tennis courts. They even pack a gourmet box lunch for you if you go for an all-day sail. I grinned. Three whole weeks without a single garbanzo bean! It sounded like heaven.

Megan tied her shoelaces hastily and stood up. "Listen," she said, "how about going downtown with me tomorrow? I want to get a perm since we'll be in the water so much these next few weeks."

"Sure," I replied, folding the green and white top and throwing it onto the stack of things I'd have to pack. "Let me know what time."

There was a knock at the door, and my mother stuck her head in the room. She looked very excited. "Tabby, have you got a minute? I need to talk to you about—" Then

5

she saw Megan. "Oh, hi," she said. "I'm sorry to interrupt. I didn't know you were still here."

"Hi, Mrs. Ellsworth," Megan said. "That's okay. I was just leaving." She turned to me. "Okay, then, tomorrow morning for the perm. And we can go to the mall, too. My brother squirted catsup on my white shorts so I need some new ones." With a cheerful wave, she scampered out the door and headed down the stairs.

My mother surveyed my room. "Are you planning to pack your entire closet?" she said mildly, staring at the clothes on the bed and the shoes piled in the middle of the floor.

"Almost," I said. "Listen, Mother, do you think I could borrow your blue garment bag? I can't get everything I need into two suitcases, even if Sail-Away does have a laundry."

Mother sat down on the corner of my bed and crossed her legs. In her jeans and plaid shirt, with her dark hair tied back in a ponytail, she seemed very young for a mother. I could see how much we looked alike. Sometimes, when we go out together, people mistake us for sisters. I've always thought that was funny, actually, and so has Mother. But right now, she really looked young; she had a sparkly look in her eyes, and I could tell that something was up.

"That's what I want to talk to you about, Tabitha," she said. "Camp."

I frowned. When my mother calls me Tabitha, something I'm probably not going to like a whole lot is usually brewing. "What is it?" I asked with a sinking feeling. "Is something wrong with my registration?"

Mother shook her head. "No, no. Tabby, you remember that Pete and Joan bought Camp Cherokee this year?"

"Oh," I said, relaxing a little. *That* camp. I'd thought for a minute that there was some sort of hitch in my going to Sail-Away, even though we'd already sent the deposit and they'd written to tell me how glad they were that I was coming and to please bring the rest of the money with me.

"Sure," I said. "I remember." I picked up a blue blouse and looked at it critically. "It's a camp for rich kids, isn't it? They're supposed to learn how to rough it out in the woods, away from modern conveniences like indoor plumbing and television and soda machines." The blue blouse had a hole in the sleeve, so I hung it back in my closet.

Mother nodded. "Right. Except that they *do* have indoor plumbing. The bathrooms are in the woods, that's all."

"Fantastic," I said sarcastically, pulling out another hanger. My red blouse had a button missing. It went back into the closet, too. "I guess that means they flush, huh?" Whenever I read about the outdoor toilets they used to have in the pioneer days, I was glad that modern technology had given us indoor plumbing.

Mother nodded again. "Their first camp session of the season ended today," she went on, watching me carefully.

"I hope it went okay," I replied, looking for my blue belt. Pete and Joan weren't exactly novices when it came to dealing with kids. Pete had been a wilderness guide for a boys' camp when he was in college and Joan was a child psychologist, so the kid part of running Camp Cherokee ought to have been easy for them. And they probably thought it was terrific that their indoor toilets were out in the woods. As I said, they're pretty adventurous people.

"Yes, it did," my mother said. "But now they've got a big problem—*two* big problems, to be precise." She stopped. "What *are* you looking for, Tabby? Are you listening?"

I was down on my hands and knees peer-

8

ing under the bed. "My blue belt," I said. "And yes, I'm listening."

Mother stood up and glanced behind her. "Is this it?" she asked. She'd been sitting on it.

"Thanks," I said, taking the belt and adding it to the stack of things on the dresser that I needed to pack in my case.

"As I said," Mother continued pointedly, sitting back down, "they've got *two* problems, and they have to solve them before the next camp session begins."

I sighed. It was obvious that Mother really wanted to talk about this. I stopped trying to pack and sat down on the floor to listen. "So they've got two problems," I prompted.

"Right," Mother replied. "They need a cook and a counselor." She paused. "Their previous cook thought that everything had to be fried and smothered with gravy, so Joan decided they had to find somebody to design a nutritional program for them and cook healthy meals. That's when Pete thought of me."

"Thought of *you*? You're going to *cook* at Camp Cherokee?"

"What do you think?"

"I think it's great," I replied enthusiastically. "I mean, I won't be around for three weeks. And you've got some vacation time coming, haven't you?" I grinned. "I'm sure the kids will *adore* your tofu burgers and corn pudding."

"So you think I should do it," Mother said slowly. She tilted her head sideways, considering.

"I really think you should do it," I said firmly. "You'll love the mountains and the clean air and the cool breeze and— "

Mother looked pleased. "You don't know how *glad* I am to hear you talk that way, Tabby."

"I think," I said, getting even more worked up, "that it will be great for you to get away from Washington. The city's so hot and humid in August, and you'll love the outdoors." I sniffed. "I can smell it now—fresh pine needles. And I can almost hear the mountain stream rushing over the—"

My mother leaned forward. "Actually, they need *two* people," she said significantly.

I gave her a blank look.

"A cook *and* a counselor, remember? That's why they thought of *both* of us. Me to cook, you to counsel. For the next two-week session."

I sat up straight. "Now wait a minute,

Mother," I said hastily. "I'm already going to camp, remember? Megan and I have paid our deposits at Sail-Away and we're leaving in six days."

"I'm sure that Sail-Away would return your deposit. Especially when we tell them it's a family emergency."

"But it's *not* an emergency," I said, beginning to panic. "I'm sure that Pete and Joan can find somebody else for the job. They just haven't looked hard enough, that's all."

"They've been looking very hard, Tab, and they're really getting desperate. They need a counselor who can also teach art and music to the kids. You could take your guitar, of course, and you'd have a chance to do some of the crafts you've been talking about. They're planning to pay us what they pay the rest of the staff, so you'd probably earn enough for that telephone you want so badly. And as you said, it would be *wonderful* to be in the mountains, with the fresh, pine-scented mountain air"—she sniffed—"and the deer and the raccoon. And we'd be there *together*, too. Wouldn't that be fun?"

I shuddered. Going to a rustic back-to-nature camp deep in a wilderness full of wild animals, with my *mother* and a bunch of spoiled rich kids? This had to be a bad joke.

"You forget," I reminded her, "how I feel about wild animals."

I have many good traits, but I am definitely *not* very brave when it comes to animals. Dogs and cats are fine. And zoo animals are okay, too, because there is a set of metal bars between them and me. But animals in the wild are another matter altogether. In fact, I find them very intimidating, without somebody's hand on the other end of a leash. This nervousness is probably a result of growing up in the city, I suppose.

"I'm sure that wild animals aren't a problem at Camp Cherokee," my mother said. "It *is* a settled area, after all." She stood up. "I think it would be fun, Tabby," she added wistfully. "And it's only for two weeks."

"No, thanks," I said firmly. I stood up also and began to hunt for my blue earrings. "You go to Cherokee and have fun for two weeks. *I'll* go to Sail-Away and have fun for *three* weeks. That way we'll both be happy."

Mother sighed. "I understand your dilemma, Tabby," she said quietly. "I know you've been looking forward to going to Sail-Away with your friend, and if you decide to stick with your plans, that's okay. I'm sure Pete and Joan will understand." She turned to go and then turned back again, giving me one of her very serious mother-to-daughter looks. "But will you at least consider the matter for a few hours? They really need your help, and I know you'd do a first-rate job with the girls. I told Pete we'd call them back tonight with our answer."

Feeling cornered, I nodded slowly. "I guess so." But after she left, I went back to my packing.

"Never," I muttered as I finally found my earrings and started to hunt for my blue scarf. "Never, never, never!"

Chapter Two

"You're *what*?" Megan stopped mixing the cookie batter to stare at me. "You mean, you and your mother *both*? I don't believe it."

"Neither do I," I said glumly, pulling up a kitchen stool. It was true. I couldn't believe I'd given in, without even a shot being fired.

"But why?" There was a dazed look on Megan's face. "I mean, we've been looking forward to Sail-Away for so long." She dropped her voice. "Did she *threaten* you?"

I shook my head. "Of course not. You know my mother doesn't do stuff like that. But I thought about the terrible bind that Uncle Pete and Aunt Joan are in, and I really didn't have a lot of choice. I could go to Sail-Away and feel like a miserable, no-good heel for

14

three weeks. Or I could go to Camp Cherokee and just feel miserable for two weeks." I picked up the spoon Megan had put down on the counter and licked it. She was making my favorite—chocolate cookies.

"But Tabby, you can't change your mind!" Megan wailed. "We've already paid our deposits and gotten our train tickets and *everything*!"

"I know." There was a big lump in my throat that even Megan's chocolate cookies couldn't soothe. "But they were really nice about my deposit. They said I could have it all back because we called before the deadline. And since Camp Cherokee's session is only two weeks long, I'll be able to get to Sail-Away for the last week."

"But our *plans*!" There were big tears in Megan's eyes. "How am I going to manage without you for two weeks, in a strange place with no friends? And you'll have a horrible time at Camp Cherokee. It doesn't even have real bathrooms!"

"I feel pretty bad about it," I said. "But you'll make new friends at Sail-Away. You'll probably meet some nice guys, too."

Megan brightened a bit. "I guess." She got a clean spoon from the drawer and began to drop little mounds of dough onto a cookie sheet. "But I'll still miss you," she added mournfully. "We were going to have so much fun together."

"Well," I said, trying to make the best of things, "we'll still have fun. It just won't be for three whole weeks, that's all. I mean, you'll still get to go sailing and swimming and play volleyball and lie in the sun and all that stuff. And I'll . . ." My voice trailed off.

Megan looked at me. "What *will* you be doing, anyway?"

"I'm going to be a counselor," I replied. "I'll live in a bunkhouse with seven little girls. I'll teach arts and crafts and music—"

"Well, *that* should be fun, anyway," Megan said, sticking the filled cookie sheet in the oven. "You've been taking guitar lessons for a long time, and your art always wins in the shows at school."

"Yeah," I said. "And Uncle Pete says they've got canoes, and a place to swim in the lake, and they take hikes through the woods, and—"

"Are there any guys?" Megan always gets to the point right away.

I sighed. "Sure. A whole bunch. All between eight and eleven."

Megan gave me a sympathetic look. "Oh," she said. "You poor thing. But I guess it wouldn't matter much, even if there *were* guys. I mean, your mother will be there telling you what to do." She shuddered. "I can't imagine going to camp with *my* mother."

That was the other thing. The idea of spending two entire weeks in a primitive mountain cabin with seven bratty girls was bad enough. But the thought of going to camp with my mother made *me* shudder, too. Even though I love her a lot and think she's a pretty neat mother on the whole, camp was invented to give kids a *vacation* from their parents. So even though I'd given in on going to Camp Cherokee, I'd put my foot down about one thing.

"Yeah," I told Megan. "But I've made Mother swear on her favorite vegetarian cookbook that she won't *act* like my mother and she won't tell anybody we're related. Aunt Joan and Uncle Pete have promised not to tell, either. Mother and I are going incognito." Uncle Pete had laughed when he heard my condition, but Aunt Joan said she understood. I kind of expected she would, since she *is* a psychologist.

Megan laughed. "It's a good idea, Tab. But

I doubt that your mother can pull it off. I've got this theory about mothers. They were born knowing how to tell people to pick up their rooms or stop making weird noises or finish their vegetables. It's in their genes. You can't ask them to change overnight. You'll think your mother is doing pretty well, and then suddenly she'll tell you to stay off the high board or be sure and wear your raincoat. It'll completely blow your cover."

"You're probably right," I agreed. "But she's promised to try, anyway."

Megan put the second tray of cookies into the oven. There was still a big gob of chocolate cookie dough left in the bowl. "What are you going to do with that?" I asked, feeling hungry.

Megan got out another spoon. "What do you think I'm going to do with it?" she replied.

"But I thought you were going to stop eating for six days."

"I changed my mind," Megan said, digging into the dough. "It probably wouldn't help much, anyway." She held out the bowl. "Dig in!"

"I love this stuff," I said. My mother doesn't make chocolate cookies with real chocolate—she uses something called carob. The cookies are brown and crunchy, but that's where the resemblance ends. I wondered what the kids at camp would say when they bit into Mother's carob cookies.

I sighed. I'd be stuck in the wilderness, with only the bugs, a bunch of little kids, and Mother's cooking for company. I reached for the bowl. "I'm going to enjoy this while I can," I said sadly.

"Are you *sure* you want to do it this way, Tabitha?" my mother asked. She had pulled up the car in front of the bus station in a dusty little town about thirty miles from Camp Cherokee. We'd driven most of yesterday and stayed at a motel last night. "I don't understand why you want to ride the bus. We could just as easily go on to the camp together."

I checked my purse to be sure I had money for the bus fare. "I've already *told* you," I said patiently. "This way nobody will see us coming in together and think we're related."

Mother frowned. "Well, yes, I understand that, but I still don't see why we can't arrive in the same car. People *do* carpool, you know. Even if they're unrelated."

"I'm not taking any chances." I got out of the car and went around to the trunk. Mother got out also to help me with my duffel bag.

"I hope you remembered to bring plenty of sunscreen," she said. "You know how easily you burn."

I suddenly recalled what Megan had said about mothers having mothering genes. "Listen, Mother," I said, "you haven't forgotten what we agreed, have you? You won't do anything that might give us away?"

"Oh, no," Mother said hurriedly, pulling out the old brown canvas duffel bag that was left over from her college days. We'd tossed for the new blue suitcase, and she'd won. "I promised, didn't I? From this instant on, I won't say a word that would give anybody a clue that you're my daughter." She glanced at her watch. "You'd better hurry, honey, or you'll miss that ten o'clock bus. Here—give me a kiss. Do you have the money for your ticket?"

I sighed as Mother pulled away from the station, waving furiously. I guessed mothering genes could be difficult to overcome.

The ten o'clock bus was late. By an hour and ten minutes to be exact. When I got tired of looking at people, I bought a magazine, and when I got sick of reading, I bought a bag of salted peanuts. At home, my mother always buys the *un*salted kind. The bus finally wheezed into the station at ten after eleven, just as I was finishing the peanuts. The driver took my ticket and threw my duffel bag into the luggage compartment. I climbed in with my guitar case and took a seat by a window.

The ride took about an hour since the bus clanked to a stop at every other dinky little gas station to pick up local passengers. When I got tired of looking out the window at the boulders and the pine trees and the clinging green vines that seemed determined to smother everything, I rummaged through my purse for my nail file. That's when I ran across Megan's postcard.

The mailman had brought it just before we'd left yesterday, and I'd been in such a hurry to finish packing and get everything into the car that I'd forgotten all about it. As it turned out, Megan hadn't gone on the train after all. Instead, she'd driven to Sail-Away a few days early with a family friend for some sort of precamp outing. Anyway, she'd sent this card. On the front was this great-looking blond guy wearing trim khaki shorts and sporting a terrific tan. He was standing beside a sailboat, and behind him a bunch of kids in bathing suits were playing volleyball.

"Come to Sail-Away," the caption said, "where *everybody* has fun." I turned the card over. On the back, Megan had scrawled:

Having a wonderful time—already! I'm glad I came up early before camp started. Met two great guys on a moonlight "get-acquainted" sail. Can't wait until you get here to share them with me! The food is great, too—we had lobster for supper.
                                        Love, Megan

I'll just *bet* she couldn't wait until I got there, I thought sarcastically. She was probably tickled pink that I *wasn't* there, so she could keep both guys for herself. But almost as soon as I had the thought, I felt ashamed. I was just feeling sorry for myself because I was all alone on a smelly old bus, wheezing up a dusty mountainside, while Megan was out on a sailboat with the breeze blowing her hair and *two* good-looking guys making sure she had a wonderful time. I couldn't *wait* to join her at Sail-Away.

The bus had pulled to a stop while I was reading my card. "Hey," the driver said, looking in the rearview mirror. "You changed your mind? You're not gettin' off here after all?"

I looked out the window again. As far as I could see, there was nothing but pine trees and dense green underbrush—probably poison oak. "*This* is it?" I asked apprehensively. "Camp Cherokee?"

The driver jerked his thumb. "The road's back there, kid. You gotta walk."

He climbed out and pulled my duffel bag from the luggage compartment. I followed him off the bus and looked hopefully at the gravel road leading up the steep mountain for any sign of a car. It was dusty in the noon sun, and there wasn't a soul in sight. Mother had said she'd ask Uncle Pete to pick me up, but since the bus was late, he probably had gone back to the camp.

"How far is it to Camp Cherokee?" I asked.

The driver shrugged. "Three miles, I reckon," he said. He gave me a gold-toothed smile. "Won't take you more'n thirty or forty minutes to hike it, even if it is kind of steep."

Thirty or forty minutes! And I'd be hiking three miles up a steep, dusty mountain road, dragging a heavy duffel bag and my guitar. I was already sweating so much that my pink ruffled top was totally wilted. My jeans were stuck to my legs, and my ponytail was coming loose. By the time I got to the camp, I'd be a total wreck. But it didn't matter. There wouldn't be anybody there to see me but a bunch of kids, Uncle Pete and Aunt Joan— and my mother.

I sighed. "Thank you," I said. As the bus roared away in a cloud of blue exhaust, I felt like crying.

Crying won't help, I reminded myself. I put my leather purse over one shoulder, picked up my duffel bag—what *had* I packed in it that weighed so much?—and my guitar case and began to walk.

After about a dozen paces, the road made a sharp bend and the highway disappeared behind a wall of dense green pine trees. The air was cool and fragrant once I was into the woods, and the only sounds were the swaying of the pines and the chirping of birds. I smiled a little. Maybe this mountain life was something you could get used to.

But after I'd walked a half mile or so, my smile faded. My duffel bag felt like it was getting even heavier, the road had turned into an alpine track, and my breath was coming in short, quick pants. The woods were dense and shadowy on both sides and filled with heaps of jagged boulders. It occurred to me that it would be the perfect place for wild animals to lurk on their way to lunch. It was definitely not a comforting thought.

Suddenly I heard a heavy crackling in the underbrush off the road. It was the sound of twigs breaking—twigs and *branches.* Goose bumps popped up on my arms, and I shivered. Could it be a mountain lion? A bear? I decided that the best thing to do was to keep walking, very steadily and quietly, and pretend that I didn't hear anything. If I didn't bother *it,* whatever it was, maybe it wouldn't bother me. So I put my head down and kept on trudging, ignoring the unmistakable sound of animal feet on the road behind me.

Just when I'd decided that I couldn't ignore the sound any longer and that it was time to *run,* a woolly head poked over my shoulder and began to lick my cheek with a very wet, sandpapery tongue.

Chapter Three

It was too late to run. I dropped my duffel bag and whirled around. Behind me stood a four-legged creature about six feet tall with a longish nose and ears. It definitely wasn't a mountain lion or a bear. Actually, it looked sort of like a camel, with a soft, woolly brown coat and large brown eyes. It didn't appear to be dangerous, but it was leaning forward, about to lick me again—probably tasting me to see whether I'd be suitable for lunch. Scared, I smacked it right across the nose with my leather purse. The woolly creature backed up and stared at me reproachfully.

"Hey!" came an indignant voice from the woods. "Stop that! You'll hurt her! Don't you know about cruelty to animals?"

There was more crackling of underbrush, and then this guy stepped out onto the road. I swallowed. He was probably the best-looking boy I'd ever seen—and in Washington, the streets are full of handsome guys. He was wearing a battered brown Indiana Jones hat, and under it his hair was thick and sort of butterscotch colored. He had on jeans, a T-shirt with CAMP CHEROKEE across the front, and scuffed leather hiking boots. As far as I was concerned, he looked just about perfect. I was suddenly very conscious of my sweat-stained pink top and my unraveling ponytail.

The boy came up to the woolly creature and put his arm around its neck. "It's okay, Lucille," he crooned, throwing me a stern look. He patted Lucille's nose. "It's all right. She made a mistake, that's all. Don't be scared."

"Now, wait just a minute!" I demanded. Even if he *was* almost perfect, I had to stand up for myself. "It seems to me that *I'm* the one who has a right to be scared. I was walking along the road, minding my own business, when all of a sudden this—this beast—charged out of the bushes and tried to take a bite out of me. I mean, why *shouldn't* I hit it?"

The boy looked offended. "She's not a beast,

she's a llama," he said. "And you don't need to be scared because llamas don't bite. Right, Lucille?" He patted the animal's camellike nose, and it lowered its head and playfully rubbed its ears against his arm. "I raised her myself, on a bottle. She's extremely affectionate. That's why she licked you. It's her way of saying hello."

"Oh," I said, clearing my throat. It was the first time I'd had the honor of being licked by a llama, and I wasn't sure I wanted it repeated. I also thought that Lucille should find another way to say hello to strangers. I didn't think it was a good idea to tell the boy that, though, since it was plain that he was very fond of her. So I said, "Well, now that we've been introduced, maybe she won't feel the need to lick me again."

The boy gave me an appraising glance, and I nervously brushed the damp hair away from my face. I could understand Lucille's crush on him. With a little encouragement, I could have one as well. "You're Tabitha, aren't you?" the boy asked.

"Tabby," I replied automatically. I picked up my duffel bag and my guitar. "Am I going the right way to get to Camp Cherokee?"

He took my duffel bag out of my hands.

"Yep. It's just up the mountain a ways. By the way, I'm Dean. Pete sent me to meet you at the highway an hour or so ago, but your bus was late. Joan's got the truck right now, so I brought Lucille down the trail to get you and your stuff."

"Thanks," I said, glancing quickly at the llama. Lucille was wearing a leather arrangement cinched around her middle, with something that looked like an upside-down sawhorse tied on top of it. I eyed it apprehensively. It was the most uncomfortable-looking saddle I'd ever seen. "You mean I'm supposed to ride to camp?" I asked weakly. I'd never been on a horse, let alone a llama.

Dean broke into a guffaw. "Are you kidding?" He boosted my duffel bag across the sawhorse legs and tied it firmly. "Llamas are pack animals. Nobody rides them." He didn't add, "you dummy," but he might as well have. "You're from the city, huh?" he went on, as if that fact explained my odd behavior. It was obvious that he didn't think much of city girls who whacked llamas with purses to ward off a few harmless licks.

"I'm from Washington," I said. "I'm going to be a counselor at Cherokee." Dean had already set off up the road, carrying my guitar, with Lucille ambling happily behind him. I hurried to catch up. "Unc—Pete just hired me for the second session." I bit my tongue. We hadn't even gotten to the camp yet and I'd almost given my identity away.

Dean looked at me. "You know," he said reflectively, "I don't understand why Pete had to go all the way to the city to hire a counselor. You'd think he'd find somebody who knows her way around the woods."

I lengthened my stride to match his, trying to look like somebody who knew her way around the woods. "I've been to camp," I said defensively. "I went to Girl Scout day camp two years ago. They taught us how to paddle a canoe and build fires and tie knots." I could have kicked myself when I realized what I'd said. Here I was, trying to sound like Daniel Boone to impress this guy, who happened to be the cutest boy I'd ever seen. I had to admit, however, that I wasn't making much headway. Dean obviously wasn't impressed.

"Well, then," Dean said with a grin, "I guess we'll make you responsible for tying all the knots in camp." Behind him, Lucille was making a nasal humming sound, like an off-key kazoo.

"What's she making that noise for?" I asked

warily, glancing over my shoulder. Maybe Lucille was getting ready to take another lick.

"Llamas hum when they're feeling good," Dean replied. We walked the rest of the way in silence.

"So *you're* Tabitha," Uncle Pete greeted me heartily, coming out of the little cabin that served as the camp office. Just then Aunt Joan pulled up in a battered pickup truck, and he called out to her. "Joan, come on over here and meet our new counselor!"

Aunt Joan—*Joan*, I corrected myself mentally—was short and athletic looking, with a warm, sweet smile. She held out her hands. "We're so glad you're here, Tabby," she said. "Now our staff is complete. Our new nutritionist just got here a couple of hours ago." She gave me a significant smile, which I took to mean that she was playing our game, and I squirmed uncomfortably.

"You've met Dean already, I see," Pete said. "And Lucille."

"Yes," I said. I certainly had.

"We kept Dean as our senior counselor when we bought the place," Pete said. "He's been at Camp Cherokee for how long, Dean?"

Dean grinned and tipped his hat back on

his head. It was the first time I had seen him really smile. He had a dimple in one cheek, I noticed. "Three, I guess," he replied. He turned the grin on me. "I used to work for the old owner. Camp Cherokee is practically my second home. I've learned a lot here."

"That's nice," I said, and then I felt silly for saying something so unimaginative. But with those gorgeous brown eyes looking at me, it was hard to come up with anything very complicated.

"Dean's *first* home is on the other side of the mountain," Joan explained. "He's a local boy. And a good thing for us," she added. "He knows all about the woods, the animals, that sort of thing. We rely on him a lot."

At that moment my mother came around the corner of the cabin. She stopped when she saw me and started to say something.

Joan stepped forward. "Marge," she said to my mother, "our new counselor, Tabby, has just arrived. I'd like you to meet her." To me, she said smoothly, "Tabby, this is Marge. She's our cook and nutritionist."

Mother held out her hand. "Hello, Tabby," she said. The corners of her mouth were twitching. "I hope you had a good trip."

"Hello, uh, Marge," I said, with a strained

smile. I felt very uncomfortable calling my mother by her first name. I had a friend once whose mother insisted that everybody—including her daughter—call her by her first name. I always felt funny when I did it, as if I were breaking some sort of unwritten rule. I usually wound up not calling her anything. After I'd said hello to my mother, I couldn't think of anything else to say without giving us both away, so I just stood there feeling awkward.

"Well," Pete said after a minute, "I'd better get back to work if I want to be ready when all those kids show up this afternoon."

"I've made a late lunch for the staff," my mother said, looking pleased. It was obvious that she was having fun already. "Raisin-and-carrot sandwiches and cottage cheese."

Joan beamed. Dean looked surprised. I wondered how he would look when he tried my mother's pumpkin soufflé. Pete glanced at his watch.

"How about lunch in thirty minutes?" he asked. "We can have our first staff meeting then, too." He looked at Dean. "In the meantime, Dean, why don't you show Tabby around the camp? She can leave her stuff in her bunkhouse. And see if you can round up the other counselors for our lunch meeting, okay?"

He went back into the office, and Joan and my mother disappeared together around the corner of the cabin, talking happily about food.

Dean and I wandered off, with Lucille padding along behind us. "This is Camp Cherokee," Dean said. He gestured around the clearing that had been cut into the pine trees. There were a few scattered clusters of small log buildings, and through the trees at one side of the clearing I could see the shimmer of a lake. It all looked very rustic—not at all like the pictures of Sail-Away in the shiny brochure they'd sent me. For a fleeting moment, I wondered what Megan was doing right then. Probably playing tennis on a spiffy green court in the middle of a manicured lawn— against a very handsome opponent.

"The camp was established five years ago," Dean was saying, "to give children from the city a chance to experience the challenges of wilderness life. It's built on the site of a Cherokee village that flourished here long before the white man colonized the area." It sounded like part of a speech he had memorized. I figured he'd had to give lots of guided tours to parents and kids during the last three years.

"Over there," Dean went on, pointing toward a large log building, "is the dining and assembly hall. On the other side is the arts-and-crafts cabin."

"That's where I'll be teaching?" I asked, stretching my neck for a better look.

"Right," Dean said. He pointed in the other direction, where I could see some stacked hay bales. "That's the archery range. We play stickball over there."

"What about tennis?" I asked, thinking of Megan again. Maybe I could polish up my backhand in my spare time, so that I'd be in top shape when I got to Sail-Away. Maybe Dean played tennis, too, I thought hopefully. If we played together, he'd definitely be impressed with my serve, which I'd been working on all summer.

But Dean was shaking his head. "The kids get plenty of opportunities to play tennis back home," he said, as if he'd answered that question dozens of times. "At Cherokee, we don't have any tennis or golf pros. The kids spend their time swimming, canoeing, going on wilderness hikes, and learning to do things the way the Indians and the pioneers did them. Our job is to be sure that every kid learns some new skill well enough to make him or her feel important."

"Of course," I said hastily. "It all sounds very—challenging." Behind us, Lucille made a noise that sounded like a laugh.

Dean looked at me. "It *is* challenging," he said quietly, dropping the canned-speech tone. "I mean, most of these kids come from really rich families, but that doesn't necessarily mean they're *privileged* kids. Most of the time, their parents are too busy to spend any *real* time with them. Or sometimes it goes the other way: they're so protective that the kids have a hard time figuring out how to do things on their own."

"I see," I said. "We're supposed to help them learn to be independent."

Dean nodded. "When these kids come here, some of them are very shy and withdrawn, while others are super aggressive, always trying to get your attention. But deep down inside, very few of the kids really have confidence in themselves and their abilities. That's where we come in. We're not just here to baby-sit, you know. A good counselor can make some pretty big changes in a kid's life, even in only two short weeks."

I felt embarrassed, and a little ashamed. During the last week, when I'd known I was coming to Camp Cherokee, I hadn't given much thought to being a counselor—or at least, to being the kind of counselor Dean was talking about. I'd been too busy feeling miserable about not going to Sail-Away with Megan, or thinking what a drag it would be going to camp with my mother. But Dean had obviously given a lot of consideration to the importance of being a good counselor. It was just one more thing I had to admire about him. The list was getting longer every minute.

"And this," Dean said, as we came to the end of a pine-needle-covered path, "is your bunkhouse."

"But it doesn't have any walls!" I blurted out, stopping to stare at the building. It was small, just long enough to hold two rows of four cots each, and the walls were built only halfway up to the roof. The openings in the walls, fortunately, were screened.

"You don't need walls," Dean said. He put a hand on my shoulder and pointed toward the eaves. "See those rolled-up awnings? If it rains, you just pull them down, like a big tent, and everybody stays dry."

"Oh," I said, "I get it." I stood there, feeling the weight of Dean's fingers on my shoulder, and my heart skipped a beat or two.

Lucille bleated again, and Dean turned away from me. "Tired of carrying that duffel bag, Lucille?" he asked, pulling it loose from the packsaddle. Lucille began to browse her way back down the path, and Dean and I went into the bunkhouse.

"Which cot do you want?" he asked.

"The one by the door, I guess," I replied. Dean dumped the duffel bag and my guitar case onto the cot while I looked around the bunkhouse. Each of the cots had clean sheets, blankets, pillows, and towels stacked neatly at the foot. In just a few hours, seven lively little girls would be living here, and I would be their counselor. For the first time, I thought about *them*, and my stomach began to feel a little queasy. What would they be like? Would I be a good counselor? Suddenly I wasn't so sure. I'd never done anything like this in my life. Tying a few knots at Girl Scout day camp didn't exactly qualify me for *this*.

Dean gave me a sympathetic look, as if he'd guessed what I was thinking. "Don't worry," he said. "We all get the willies before the kids show up. After they're settled in and you get acquainted with them, you'll be fine. And if you need any help, be sure to let me know." He threw me a grin, and the dimple flashed again in his cheek. "I get paid extra to be senior counselor."

Outside I heard the sound of voices, and I followed Dean out the door. Two kids, a girl and boy about my age, were standing on the path. The boy had flaming red hair and freckles and a big, lopsided grin. The girl was petite and blond and very pretty.

"Hi," the girl greeted me. "Are you the new counselor?"

"Tabby," Dean said, "this is Heidi, the other girls' counselor. Her bunkhouse is over to the left behind those trees. And this is Randy. The boys' bunkhouses are on the other side of the camp."

Heidi gave me a friendly smile. "I hope you like it here," she said. "Pete was really worried about finding somebody who could do crafts. It was great that you could come on such short notice."

"Yeah," Randy said, grinning. "Especially after what happened to the last counselor."

I frowned. "What do you mean?" Uncle Pete had told me that the counselor had left unexpectedly, but he hadn't mentioned anything *happening* to her.

"Randy," Dean said sharply, "lay off the teasing, okay?"

Randy tried to look innocent. "I didn't mean anything," he said to me, then turned to Dean. "You've got to admit that she *did* leave in kind of a hurry."

"What happened to the last counselor?" I asked Dean, beginning to panic a bit.

Dean made a face. "*Nothing*," he insisted. "It's just one of Randy's little jokes, that's all."

Heidi smiled. "He's always making jokes," she explained. "But he's harmless. You sort of have to get used to him."

"That's right," Randy agreed cheerfully, putting his arm around Heidi. "I'm not so bad then." Heidi snuggled against him, and I could see that the two of them were *very* friendly.

"Hey," Dean said suddenly, looking at his watch. "Pete told me to tell you guys that we're having a staff meeting at lunch. In about ten minutes."

"Okay," Randy said. "Maybe we'd better head over to the dining hall now." We all turned to go, and halfway down the path Randy glanced back over his shoulder at me. "Just stay away from the lake," he warned. "Especially the places where the lily pads are really thick. That's where they like to hide."

"Where *who* likes to hide?" I asked, confused.

Randy's eyes were round and serious. "The alligators," he replied in a loud whisper. "They're particularly ferocious between the hours of twelve and four in the afternoon. They'll eat *anything* then."

"But I've never heard of alligators this far north," I protested.

"They migrated," Randy said. "From Louisiana, just after the Civil War. Crawled all the way—"

"Randy," Dean said impatiently, "you're a great guy and all that, but would you please shut up?"

I was almost positive that Randy was joking, but I gave the lake a careful inspection as we passed it on our way to the dining hall, just in case. Fortunately there were no alligators in sight.

Chapter Four

"What's this?" Randy had lifted the top slice of bread and was staring at his sandwich with a pained expression. "Somebody forgot the baloney! This looks like carrots and raisins."

At the other end of the long, pine-topped table, my mother glanced up and smiled. "Yes, carrots and raisins are much better for you than baloney," she said. "They have lots of vitamins and iron."

I suppressed a snicker. Over the years, I'd gotten used to carrot-and-raisin sandwiches.

"Hey, I *like* baloney," Randy said in an aggrieved voice. "Our last cook always fixed baloney sandwiches."

"Our last cook," Joan said pointedly, "didn't

know very much about nutrition. Marge has studied diet and nutrition for years. I'm sure you'll enjoy her cooking after you get used to it."

My urge to snicker grew stronger. It would take a lot longer than two weeks for people to get used to some of Mother's more unusual inspirations.

Muttering under his breath, Randy took a bite of sandwich. I sneaked a look at Dean. He'd already finished his and was digging into his cottage-cheese-and-alfalfa-sprout salad as if he really liked it. If the truth be known, he was probably just hungry, but that didn't seem to matter to Mother. She was watching him, beaming. Dean was obviously a man after her own heart. Mother had good taste, I thought. Dean was a guy after *my* heart, too.

Pete pushed his empty plate away. "Is everybody set to meet the wild horde arriving this afternoon?" he asked, putting a clipboard on the table in front of him. "Let's go over our assignments, just to make sure that we're all on board the same train." I winced. Uncle Pete may have come to the wilderness, but he'd brought his Madison Avenue lingo with him.

Pete checked his list. "Dean, you'll be working with Joan in the office to check the campers in as they arrive. At last count, we had twenty-nine kids coming. Heidi and Tabby, you should probably station yourselves in your bunkhouses so you can help the girls settle in. Heidi, we've given the nine- and ten-year-olds to you. You've got a bit more experience, and the older kids can be more creative in the mischief they get into. Tabby, you'll take the sevens and eights." He handed each of us a stack of oaktag cards. "These are information cards on each camper—family background, likes, dislikes, allergies, skills, stuff like that. I hope I got all the nicknames right."

Randy grinned. "Can I take the afternoon off?"

"Not on your life," Pete said. He handed him a long sheet of paper. "Here's a list of things that need fixing. Better bring your hammer." He turned to Joan. "Okay, that's all from me for now."

Joan leaned forward with her elbows on the table, an earnest look in her eyes. "These kids are with us to have fun, and I know they will," she began. "But at the same time, we want camp to be a valuable learning experience for them. That means that you'll each have to give some thought to the special needs

44

of your campers. If you go over your information cards carefully, you may get some ideas about what those needs might be." She reached over and took up my stack of cards. "For example, Tabby has an eight-year-old named Cynthia. Her mother tells us that Cynthia likes to overdramatize things, to make up stories."

"Oh," Randy said wisely. "You mean she tells *lies*, right?" Heidi nudged him.

"They're probably not lies, really," Joan replied smoothly. "Kids often overdramatize to make themselves feel more powerful."

"Powerful?" I asked doubtfully.

"Sure," Joan said. "They often feel that they don't have enough *control* over their lives, especially if they have very protective parents. So they try to exert control through their imaginations. The wilder the stories, the better, of course."

I bit my lip. Joan was describing just the kind of kid I didn't need on my first job as counselor.

"You might try practicing a little psychology on Cynthia, Tabby," Joan went on. "For instance, you might let her take charge of some of the activities. Maybe then she won't need to dramatize so much. If she gets recognition for doing something well, she might feel more sure of herself."

"It doesn't sound easy," I said.

"It isn't," Heidi answered. "But you'll get the hang of it after a session or two."

I shuddered. I wasn't planning to come back for another session, no matter how good-looking Dean was. In fact, I was planning to break out of this place as quickly as possible, in order to get to Sail-Away for some *fun*, maybe even before the session ended. But nobody here knew that, of course.

"Listen," Dean said, "the really hard part is when the kids get homesick. The trick there is to distract them right away."

"Right," Heidi chimed in. "For some of them, this is their first time away from home, and they're in very strange surroundings. A lot of the city kids have a hard time sleeping in the bunkhouses unless the awnings are down. That way they can't hear the night noises, especially the owls."

I don't blame them, I thought fervently. I wasn't so sure about those night noises myself.

Randy smiled at me. "Yeah, you've got to watch out for those owls, Tabby," he said helpfully. "There are these little holes in the roof, and sometimes the owls squeeze into the bunkhouses at night and fly around, flapping in people's faces and going *whoo-whoo*." He stuck his hands under his arms and began flapping his elbows like wings. "Bats, too," he added.

Oh no. Bats were at the top of the list of animals I hated most in the world.

"Randy," Joan said reprovingly, "you *know* there aren't any owls or bats in the bunkhouses."

"But I did see one," Randy objected. "In Tabby's bunkhouse. I was only trying to warn her."

"If you really saw an owl in there," Dean spoke up, "you'd better get your hammer and some extra shingles and plug that hole. We don't need that kind of trouble."

I threw Dean a grateful look. I could see why he'd gotten to be senior counselor.

Pete stood up. "I know you all probably have lots of questions, but why don't we hold them until later? Don't forget about the all-camp assembly tonight after supper, down by the lake. We'll have another staff meeting after breakfast to talk about the way things are going."

"And if you run into any unexpected problems," Joan added, "just let me know. I'll be glad to help you work them out."

I started to push my chair back and stopped. Something large and furry was rubbing against my ankle. I looked down to see a strange black animal, far too large to be a cat, with a pretty white stripe down its—

"Skunk!" I cried, scrambling frantically up on my chair. "There's a *skunk* in here!"

"A skunk!" Randy said delightedly. "Hey, Dean, get the gun! Tabby's treed a skunk!" He looked at me as I teetered on the chair, and he began to laugh. "Nope, correction—the skunk's treed Tabby."

"It's okay, Tabby," Heidi said comfortingly. "It's only Lilac."

"Lilac?"

Dean bent over to pick up the skunk. "Lilac," he explained, "is one of our mascots."

I looked at Lilac, who was nuzzling Dean's ear. "But doesn't he—?"

"Lilac's been de-skunked," Pete said. "He's odor-free."

Sheepishly I climbed down from the chair. "Sorry," I muttered. I glanced at Dean, who had walked off with the skunk trailing along behind him like a fat black and white cat. First Lucille, now Lilac, I thought, shaking my head. I might as well give up. I'd *never* be able to impress Dean.

I spent the next hour reviewing my campers' information cards, trying to memorize the kids' backgrounds. Suzie had a weight problem and was supposed to be watching her diet—but that wouldn't be a problem, at least not with Mother's cooking. Linda was allergic to ragweed, and Mandy had to be careful of poison ivy. Ginger was afraid of the dark, and when she was nervous, her mother reported, she had to go to the bathroom frequently. They all seemed more or less normal. I looked at Cynthia's card again and sighed, wondering how to deal with her tendency to overdramatize.

When I had learned as much as I could from the cards, I went over to the crafts cabin and looked through the supplies, trying to figure out which of them we could use. Pinecone crafts would be easy, and so would leafprinting. There were easels and paints, clay for modeling or making pots, drawing pencils and sketch pads, construction paper and scissors, and a big box of odds and ends. Maybe tomorrow we could get some brown paper bags from the kitchen and make Indian masks. I didn't think we'd run out of things to do.

"Hey, Tab!" It was Heidi. "The first car has just arrived! Come on—we'd better get over to the bunkhouses!"

I'm not ready! I thought in a panic as I dashed back to the bunkhouse. Hurriedly I changed into a clean blue blouse and added a ribbon to my ponytail. Then I began to pace, wondering for the hundredth time why I had agreed to do this.

Within two hours, all the campers had arrived and were noisily getting acquainted. Linda and Hallie, both redheads, were sitting on Linda's cot, leafing through a scrapbook that Hallie had brought. Suzie, who looked as if she could lose ten pounds without noticing that they were gone, was unpacking her second suitcase. Where was she going to put all of that stuff? Carol and Mandy were outside catching grasshoppers and stuffing them into an empty Coke bottle. Ginger, the youngest and smallest of the bunch, had fastened onto me and wouldn't turn me loose. Cynthia, my "problem child," wasn't doing anything at the moment. She was sitting on her cot, her arms folded across her chest, staring sulkily off into space. I could see that she was tall for eight, and fairly athletic looking. I thought it might be a good idea if we got acquainted, but first I'd have to do something about Ginger.

"Ginger," I said, "wouldn't it be nice if you went over and helped Suzie unpack?"

Ginger put a thumb into her mouth. That surprised me. Ginger must be going into second grade, at least. "I don't want to," she said, talking around her thumb. She put her other hand in mine. "I want to stay with you."

"But you didn't come here to stay with me," I reminded her. "You came to camp to make new friends."

"*You're* my friend," Ginger said, squeezing my hand even harder. "Don't you like me?" she asked worriedly.

I knelt down. "Of course I like you," I replied. Then I leaned forward to whisper in Ginger's ear. "But Suzie looks terribly lonesome, unpacking all by herself. Don't you think *she* needs a friend? Won't you go help her?"

Ginger looked at Suzie for a minute, considering, before she took her thumb out of her mouth. "Well, I guess," she said grudgingly.

"Good!" I beamed at her.

After Ginger was safely involved with Suzie, I turned away and went over to Cynthia. "Hi," I said brightly. "All settled?"

Cynthia didn't say anything. Her face was screwed into a pouty scowl that looked as if it might be permanent, and her two blond braids stuck out belligerently on either side. She *looked* like a problem child.

I sat down beside her on the cot. "Is there anything I can help you with?" I asked.

Cynthia still remained silent.

I waited for a minute and then stood up. "Well, if you think of anything," I said, turning away, "I'll be glad to—"

"I didn't want to come," Cynthia said sullenly. "She made me."

"Who?"

"My mom. She always makes me do things I don't want to."

I laughed a little. "I know," I said sympathetically. "Mothers are like that."

Cynthia looked at me suspiciously. "Is yours?"

"Absolutely," I replied, sitting back down on the bed. "But I fool her."

Cynthia straightened a bit. "How do you do that?"

I grinned. "Well, I forget all about her and have a good time anyway." It felt funny to be talking about my mother like that, especially when it wasn't exactly true, but at least Cynthia was listening.

"Yeah, maybe," she said. "But I *still* don't like being here"—she looked around the bunkhouse—"with all these babies." She stuck out her chin. "I'd rather be in with the bigger kids."

Ginger came up. Her thumb was back in her mouth. "Tabby, I have to go," she said.

"Go?" I asked in surprise. "But you just got here."

"No," she said urgently. "I've got to go to the *bathroom*." She looked around. "Where is it?"

"It's down the path," Cynthia said. "I already found it."

"Well, then, since you know where it is, maybe you can show her," I said. Maybe if Cynthia helped with Ginger, she'd feel more useful.

"Yeah, I guess," Cynthia said reluctantly, getting up. "Come on, Ginger." She squared her shoulders and threw me a disgusted look. "I told you," she said. "They're all babies." But she didn't sound quite so unhappy about it this time.

Dinner was chaos. Maybe there *were* only twenty-nine campers, but from the racket they were making in the dining hall, it sounded

53

like there were twenty-nine hundred. My mother—*Marge,* I reminded myself firmly— had cooked her old standby, lasagna, and even I had to admit that she'd done a pretty good job. There was also Jell-O salad and potato soup. We all lined up with trays to get our food, the way we do in the cafeteria at school.

My kids—I was still getting used to thinking about them that way—and I sat at one table. Randy and his bunch were behind us, and they were pretty rowdy. I looked around for Dean. He was on the other side of the dining hall with his campers. Heidi was there, too.

I'd just settled down to eat when somebody from Randy's table came over and stole Ginger's milk. Naturally she set up a howl, and it took a few minutes to calm her down. We'd just gotten everything straightened out and I'd gone back to my meal when I discovered something awful.

There was a dead fish in my soup.

Chapter Five

The moon was coming up over the pine trees by the time we all gathered down at the lake for Pete's "opening ceremony." We sat on the ground inside a special circle of stones that Pete called the Assembly Circle. Some of the kids were whispering that it was a *magic* circle, and I could see why they felt that way. The moon had streaked the lake with silver, and the pines cast long, dark shadows over the rocks.

When Pete got up to speak, everybody fell silent. He talked about having fun at camp and learning to be respectful and independent. I hoped that all my campers were paying strict attention. Then everybody got a candle from a box and stood in a circle while Joan played her dulcimer and sang a Cherokee song. Still wearing his Indiana Jones hat, Dean came around with a lighted candle, and we all lit our candles from his. Then we said the Camp Cherokee pledge of friendship.

It was a very nice ceremony, and I could tell that even the bigger kids were impressed. When Dean lit my candle, his fingers accidentally touched mine. I felt shivery and wonderful.

As Dean walked away, I couldn't help looking after him. I don't know whether it was the candlelight or the moonlight or what, but those definitely were romantic feelings fluttering inside me, like crazy little butterflies.

After the candlelighting, Joan played her dulcimer some more and we sang along. Mother was there—I could see her sitting on a blanket next to Pete a little way up the beach. I was perched on a rock beside the lake, watching the moon pour ripples of silver over the water. As I was wondering if I should go get my guitar and play along with Joan, Dean came and sat down beside me.

"Getting used to Camp Cherokee?" he asked casually.

I forced myself to think about something other than the way his hair grew along his neck. "If I can get used to dead fish in my soup," I said, thinking about Randy's little "joke" at dinner, "I can get used to anything."

I shivered a little, but I wasn't exactly cold. It was so romantic to be sitting in the moonlight with the cutest boy I'd ever seen. But I was very conscious of my mother, sitting where she could see exactly what was going on. Not that anything *was* going on, mind you. Obviously Dean wasn't that sort of guy. Still, there she was, and with only a turn of her head, she could see us. The thought made me pull away from him quickly. At least that way, Mother would see moonlight between us.

But Dean didn't know that Mother was my mother, so he of course wasn't worrying about whether she could see us. "You were a good sport about that fish," he said, moving closer. "I'm afraid Randy overdoes things sometimes. When a new counselor comes on the staff, he sort of appoints himself in charge of initiation rites."

"Oh," I said. It was nice to know that Dean thought I was a good sport. "What *did* happen to the last counselor?" I looked out over the lake again, but there was still no sign of alligators hiding in the lily pads.

Dean chuckled and shook his head. "It was something about her family, I think," he said. "She had to go away with her grandmother or something." He glanced at me curiously. "How did Pete find out about you?" he asked.

I looked away. "Oh, it was sort of a mutual-friend kind of thing," I said evasively. "I mean, he knew somebody who knew me." Which was the truth, even if it wasn't the *whole* truth.

Dean nodded. He was looking at a rock that he was turning over in his fingers. "Well, however it happened, I'm glad you came."

I looked back at him in surprise. "You are? I mean, after my meeting with Lucille—"

He gave me a sideways glance and a quick grin. "I guess I kind of gave you a hard time about Lucille, didn't I? You know," he added, "llamas only lick people they like a lot."

I laughed self-consciously. "I've never been licked by a llama before. And meeting Lilac was certainly an experience."

Dean grinned again. "Just wait, Tabby. You'll probably have lots of great experiences before the next couple of weeks are over." And then, as if by accident, he put his hand down on the rock between us, his fingers touching mine. A second later, he was lightly holding my hand.

Great experiences? The most awful one I could think of was sitting on a rock beside a lake in the moonlight, holding hands with the most handsome boy in the world—with my mother not ten yards away, in full view. It wasn't the hand-holding part that bothered me, of course. That was pretty wonderful, and the touch of Dean's fingers made me feel all fizzy and sparkly, like Roman candles on the Fourth of July. It was having my *mother* there that made it awful. I just couldn't stand the thought that she might look up and see us sitting there, me with a moonstruck smile on my face and Dean holding my hand.

I suddenly felt so flustered that I jerked my hand away, hard.

Dean looked at me, confused. "Hey," he said in a troubled voice. "I'm sorry. I thought—"

And suddenly, miserably, I *knew* what he'd thought. He'd thought I liked him. Now he'd think that I had been leading him on with all those smiles and glances. He'd think I was one of those silly flirts like Cookie Baxter back home. Cookie liked nothing better than to get a guy to like her, just so she could turn up her nose at him. But that wasn't the way I felt about Dean at all! I was wild about him—but there was my *mother* over there, for pity's sake! What else could I do? I sneaked a quick glance at Dean, who was sitting stiffly, looking down at his hands. I'd wrecked the whole thing, I told myself sadly. He thought I didn't like him.

I sighed. What should I do now? Should I get up and say "Excuse me for being such a jerk," and go jump in the lake? No, that wouldn't solve anything. Should I—

Suddenly there was a swish of wings just over our heads and something large, with enormous, hooked talons, landed heavily on Dean's hat. It was the biggest owl I had ever seen.

"Hey!" I cried. I jumped to my feet, waving my arms violently. "Shoo! Scat! Get out of here!"

It didn't work. The owl remained sitting on Dean's hat, its round yellow eyes blinking in the moonlight. It looked absolutely unperturbed.

Dean was unperturbed, too. "It's okay, Tabby," he said mildly. "Sit down, it's only Merlin." The owl gave a small, happy *whoo?* and hopped onto his shoulder.

"Merlin?"

The owl bent its head and delicately nibbled the tip of a wing feather with its sharp beak. I never thought I'd be glad to see an owl sitting so close to me, but I was, actually. At least Merlin's arrival had broken the awful tension between us.

Dean stroked the owl, and it hopped onto his arm. "Merlin and I are old friends. I found him in a barn a couple of years ago, when he was just a chick. He lives on his own now, in the big windfall up on Rocky Point. But every now and then he shows up at camp in the evening to remind me that we're still buddies."

I sat down again cautiously. Merlin might be *Dean's* buddy, but that beak of his was razor-sharp, and there was no guarantee that he wouldn't decide to take a nip or two out of my ear. I felt that I had every right to be a coward, at least where Merlin was concerned.

"Dean," I said warily, "are there any other animals at Camp Cherokee that I need to know about—before I meet them in person, I mean?"

Dean grinned. "Well, there *was* Blackstone," he replied. "You would have liked him, I'll bet."

I cleared my throat. "Who, or what, if I may ask, is Blackstone?"

"He was just about the cutest little bear cub you ever—"

"*Bear cub?*" I said in a strangled voice.

"—saw." Dean grinned again. "He'd always nuzzle up to people, wanting to be scratched under the collar."

"A bear with a collar?"

"Well, he got too big and rough to play with," Dean went on, "and last year we took him way up the mountain and turned him loose in the forest."

I sat back, feeling relieved. At least there was one animal I wouldn't have to worry about—

But I didn't get a chance to finish my thought. Off the shore, a dozen yards away from us, there was a large splash and the sound of somebody thrashing in the water.

"Help!" Cynthia screamed. "Hallie fell in! Save her!"

It only took a moment for Dean to jump off the rock and wade into the waist-deep water to fish Hallie out. And that was the end of our almost-magical interlude. When the rescue was over, Joan put away her dulcimer and Pete announced that it was nearly lights-out time. We all trooped to our bunkhouses, and Cynthia, in a self-important tone, re-counted for the third or fourth time how Hallie had slipped off the rock and how she had screamed for help at exactly the right time. I could see exactly what had led her mother to say that she overdramatized things.

I'd expected the girls to be so tired that they would go off to sleep without any fuss. But most of them seemed a little apprehensive about spending their first night in the woods, especially since it was too warm to leave the awnings down, except while we changed into our pajamas. Ginger was whimpering a little in her cot in the corner, and Suzie looked as if she might cry, too. I thought about what Dean had said about kids being homesick, and I wished I could think of a bedtime story that would distract them. But nothing came to mind except the really scary tales that Megan liked to tell, which would only make things worse. Why hadn't I thought of something earlier?

I had a flashlight that I was planning to use under my blanket to write a postcard to Megan. But it would take an entire letter to tell her about Lucille and Lilac and Merlin and Blackstone and *especially* Dean. I'd have to tell her about his funny hat and his butterscotch colored hair and the way he'd made Randy quit teasing and—I shut my eyes. And I'd also have to tell her that he probably thought I was a real jerk for yanking my hand away as if he were trying to chop it off or something. If I could only have explained about Mother, he might have understood. The whole thing was a mess. How was I going to fix it? I turned the problem over in my mind for a while, but I didn't get anywhere. Finally I fell asleep.

But only for about thirty seconds. The next thing I knew, an ice-cold waterfall was cascading over me. My bed and I were completely drenched, and something black and crawly was wiggling across my wet pillow.

"Aarrgh!" I was out of my cot in a split second, my pajamas dripping wet. I spit out a mouthful of water. "Snake! There's a snake in my bed!"

The girls all sat up, and somebody flipped on the light. Outside the bunkhouse, there was one snicker, then another, then a whole chorus of giggles. And inside, led by Ginger and Suzie, my campers burst into gales of laughter. Over my bed hung an upside-down bucket, and on my soaked pillow lay an innocent rubber snake.

"Randy!" I said through my teeth.

"We always baptize our new counselors, Tabby."

It was Heidi's voice, still choked with giggles. She must have brought her whole bunkhouse to stand outside in the dark and watch while Randy pulled the string that had dumped the bucket of ice-cold water onto my bed.

"Yeah," Randy said gleefully. "It's sort of a tradition at Cherokee. Now you're one of us."

I picked up a towel and began to rub my hair dry. "Thanks," I said sarcastically. "What a privilege." Then I stared at my cot, which was still dripping. "Do I also get to sleep in a wet bed for the rest of the night?"

"No," Heidi said, entering the bunkhouse with her arms full of sheets. In a minute or two my wet bedding was gone and there was a dry mattress and pillow in its place. "I hope you didn't mind this too much," she said quietly, as we finished tucking in the new sheets. "It *is* sort of a tradition."

I looked around at my campers as they started settling down for the second time that night. They seemed relaxed and ready to go to sleep. Ginger and Suzie had apparently forgotten all about being homesick. Their sniffles had vanished, and they were actually smiling. For them, the whole episode had been great fun.

"No, I don't mind," I told Heidi. "The distraction was better than a bedtime story."

As I finally drifted off to sleep, I heard the eerie *whoo-whoo* of an owl. It was probably just Merlin, I reminded myself as I turned over, remembering how terrific Dean had looked in the moonlight with the owl on his shoulder. I doubted if Sail-Away had a resident owl, not to mention a skunk and a llama that hummed like a kazoo when she was happy. And not to mention Dean. Of course, none of that mattered much now. I had really messed things up with Dean. I doubted that he'd make any attempts to be anything more than friendly now.

The next morning I began arts-and-crafts lessons for the younger kids: the boys from Randy's bunkhouse and the girls from mine. We made paper-bag Indian masks.

It wasn't exactly a spectacular artistic success. None of the kids exhibited any striking talent, unless you counted Mandy's squirrel mask, with its piece of pasted-on real fur that she'd found in the odds and ends box. Cynthia decided not to make a mask at all. Instead she painted her own face purple with blue stripes and stuck some turkey feathers into her blond braids. Her mask was very creative, I told her, but unfortunately she'd used an indelible marking pen instead of washable paints. That meant she'd be wearing her artwork for several days to come.

But it didn't seem to matter to the kids whether they had any artistic talent—they were having *fun*. After they'd finished their masks, we went out to the Assembly Circle and I played my guitar and they improvised Indian dances. Even purple-faced Cynthia joined in, and one of the boys, a little kid named Paul, was the star of the show with his acrobatic improvisations.

Just before lunch, Dean came down the hill toward us. My heart stopped when I saw him approaching. Did he want to talk to me? Of course not. He only had to tell Cynthia that there was a phone call for her in the office.

Cynthia straightened up, her good time forgotten. "Is it my mother?" she asked.

Dean nodded. "She just wants to say hello and be sure you're okay."

Cynthia shook her head stubbornly. "I *won't* talk to her," she said, her voice rising. "I won't, I won't, I *won't!*" She yanked the turkey feathers out of her braids and stamped on them. "You can't make me!"

I put down my guitar. "But she just wants

to say hello," I said in surprise. "There's nothing wrong with your mother just wanting to *talk* to you, is there?"

Cynthia looked around the circle. Everybody was watching her now. "She treats me like a little baby!" she howled, her purple and blue face all screwed up. "I'm *not* a baby! I'm going into the fourth grade! Why can't she leave me alone?!"

"But Cynthia, don't you think you're over-reacting—"

"I *hate* her!"

Obviously I wasn't saying anything to improve the situation. I threw Dean a helpless, what-do-I-do-now look, and he stepped forward.

"Listen, Cynthia," he said, putting his hand on her shoulder and lowering his voice so that she had to stop shrieking to listen. "If you ask me, I think that the real problem is that your *mom* doesn't want to be left alone."

"Huh?" Cynthia choked on a strangled half-sob. "What do you mean?"

Dean's voice was very serious. "Well, sometimes moms are upset when their kids go to camp for the first time. They worry a lot, and some of them get really lonesome."

I stared at Dean. His approach was brilliant. Cynthia had stopped crying. She was really paying attention! And the other kids were listening, too.

I couldn't get over my admiration for Dean. From the way he was handling the situation, you would have thought he'd been taking child psychology lessons from Joan.

Cynthia looked doubtful. "Do you really think it'll work?" she asked. "If I'm especially nice to her now, will she feel better and stop trying to tell me what to do?"

"Well, I wouldn't exactly guarantee it," Dean replied. "But it's worth a try, isn't it?"

Reluctantly Cynthia nodded. "I guess so," she said. "Where's the phone?" she added with a last sniffle, wiping her blue nose with the back of her hand.

"Come on, I'll show you." With a grin and a wink at me, Dean led Cynthia up the hill, holding her hand. I watched them go, wishing it were *my* hand he was holding. As long as my mother wasn't around, that is.

Chapter Six

"What I want to know," Sammy said plaintively, staring at his lunch plate, "is when we're going to get some *real* food. Like meat, for instance." Sammy was one of Randy's kids. He was eight and an incredible whiner. The day before, he'd complained about having to go swimming because the water in the lake was too cold and it tasted funny and there were turtles in it. At home they had a heated swimming pool with chlorine in it and *no* turtles.

It was the third day of camp, and so far Mother's lunches had consisted of an acre of alfalfa sprouts, a ton of homemade peanut butter, buckets of cottage cheese, and bushels of fruit. For supper we'd had vegetable lasagna, vegetable spaghetti, and vegetable enchiladas. And, of course, plenty of terrific veggie desserts: carrot cake, rice pudding, banana bread. I sighed, remembering how lucky I'd felt when I'd contemplated three weeks at Sail-Away without a single garbanzo bean. I wondered what kind of gourmet lunch Megan was eating right now.

"Yeah," one of the older boys said. "What's going on? How come we don't get hamburgers and hot dogs and stuff like that? The camp I went to last year had potato chips every day. And soda to drink."

Joan came into the dining hall with her arms full of baskets containing Mother's special nut bread. "Hamburgers?" she asked casually. "Well, sure. They're okay for *other* camps. But you decided to come to Camp Cherokee because we're special. We have food you're not likely to get everywhere else."

"But I *love* hamburgers," Suzie protested next to me. She puffed out her plump cheeks and wrinkled her nose disdainfully at the cottage cheese and sprouts on her plate. "At home I get them every day for lunch—two of them, if I want. And I get fried chicken for supper, or pizza. *This* stuff is for the birds."

"Maybe that's why birds never get fat," Cynthia suggested, not very tactfully. She giggled, and I frowned in her direction.

"My father says I'm not fat," Suzie replied defensively. "I'm naturally heavy. It runs in the family." She poked at her sprouts with her fork. "I could eat stuff like this all the time and I'd never lose any weight."

"Maybe that's because of all the candy bars she hides under her bed," Linda whispered loudly to Hallie behind her hand.

Suzie's face reddened. "What's under my bed isn't any of your business," she told Linda haughtily. She turned to me. "I think we should demand fried chicken for supper. And french fries."

"Yeah," one of Dean's boys chimed in. "That's a good idea." He pounded his fist on the table. "We want fried chicken and french fries." Someone else took up the chant, and then half the kids at the table were shouting, "We want fried chicken!" while the other half screamed, "We want french fries!"

But it wasn't going to do them any good to complain. I knew from experience that Mother didn't believe in fried chicken or french fried potatoes. She's always telling me what horrible things will happen to me if I gum up the insides of my arteries with too much fat. Of course I've been listening to Mother's sermons for years, and she's almost got me convinced, even though I made a special point to be at Megan's when they're having fried chicken for supper. But it probably wouldn't help to preach to these kids, and I can't do it as well as Mother anyway.

So I just asked, in between chants, "Hey, would you settle for pizza?"

Suzie squinted at me. "Pizza?" she asked hopefully.

"Yeah," I said loudly. "With thick crust and lots of cheese and mushrooms and a whole bunch of super toppings."

Some of the kids stopped banging on the table. "Hey," Sammy said, "that'd be terrific." He looked at me. "Do you think the cook could make it *tonight*?"

"Sure," I replied. "She *loves* to make pizza. It's her favorite thing to cook." Of course my mother's pizza would have whole-wheat crust and lots of veggies, but with all the cheese she puts on it, the kids would hardly notice.

Randy gazed at me. "So how come you know so much about the cook, Tabby? I thought you'd never met her before."

I felt my face turn beet red. "I—I haven't," I stammered. "I'm just guessing, that's all. I mean, all cooks like to make pizza, don't they?"

Randy was really staring at me now. "You know," he said thoughtfully, "now that I think of it, there's something about you that reminds me of—"

Fortunately Pete came into the dining hall right then with his clipboard under his arm. "Everybody finished eating?" he asked. "I've got some announcements, so I'd like to have your attention."

I turned my head away and fastened my eyes on Pete, hoping that Randy's attention had been distracted. The last thing in the world I needed was for him to figure out that Mother and I were related. He was such a tease; he'd never let me hear the end of it. And if Dean knew that Mother and I had come to camp together, he'd think it was because she didn't trust me or something like that. It would be perfectly humiliating.

I folded my hands and pretended to listen while Pete told everybody about the hike around the lake we were going to take that afternoon, but I was really watching Dean, on the other side of the dining hall. After that first romantic, moonlit evening—the evening I spoiled—I hadn't seen much of him except in the dining hall and at assemblies. He always seemed too busy with his campers, or with the other stuff he had to do as senior counselor, to even notice that I was around. And in the evenings, I'd been accompanying Joan's dulcimer with my guitar, so we didn't even sit together at assemblies. I knew that I might as well give up hope. Soon I'd be going back to Washington and Dean would go back to the other side of the mountain and that would be the end of it.

"Just one more thing," Pete was saying. He looked around the room. "I want to remind everybody about the rule against keeping food in the bunkhouses. Remember, you're in the woods, and the woods are full of animals. Let's not tempt them to come into the bunkhouses by leaving food where they can find it. Okay?" He looked around again. "I'll see you all at the Assembly Circle in thirty minutes for our hike."

I waited until I was sure nobody would notice and then sneaked into the kitchen. Mother was there with her sleeves rolled up, whistling cheerfully as she washed dishes.

"I'd hug you," Mother said, glancing up with a smile, "but my hands are wet."

"That's okay, Marge," I said. "We're not

supposed to be on hugging terms, anyway. Remember?"

"Oh, right," Mother said. She giggled. "It sounds so funny when you call me Marge."

"It *feels* funny when I call you Marge," I said. "But that's not what I came to talk to you about."

"You came to tell me about the near mutiny in the dining hall, huh?"

"Oh. Joan must have told you." Actually, I wanted to talk to her about Dean, too. But it wouldn't do any good.

Mother pointed with a dripping hand to the table, where she'd been chopping green peppers. "I've already got the pizzas started. Thanks for suggesting it."

"That's okay," I said.

"Are you having a good time?" Mother asked, suddenly sounding a bit anxious. "Are you glad you came?"

I thought of my campers, and the kids in my crafts class, and Dean. Even if nothing ever happened between us—and I was sure by now that nothing would—I was glad I'd met him. At least it was good to know that there were actually boys like him in the world. "Yeah," I said finally. "I'm glad."

"Well, then, so am I," Mother said, turning to her dishwashing. "Have a good hike."

"Thanks Mo— uh—Marge," I said as I headed toward the door.

The minute I entered the bunkhouse I knew there was something wrong. I'd expected everybody to be getting ready for the hike, since we were leaving in a few minutes. But instead, all the girls were gathered around Carol's cot. She had dumped the contents of her suitcase out on her bed and was angrily rummaging through the pile of clothes.

"I told you!" she cried. "They're not here! Somebody *stole* them!"

"What's not here?" I asked, coming up behind the girls. Mandy stepped aside to make room for me.

"Her earrings," Linda explained. "She's lost her blue earrings."

"My *turquoise* earrings," Carol snapped. She put both hands on her hips and whirled to glare at Linda. "And I told you, I didn't *lose* them. I left them right here on the windowsill over my bed. Somebody *took* them."

"Now, now," I said mildly, hoping to defuse what was threatening to become a pretty explosive situation. "That's a pretty serious accusation, Carol."

"Well, it's a serious crime," Carol responded hotly. "I mean, those are antique earrings. They belonged to my grandmother. They're worth a *lot* of money."

I looked around the group. Six innocent faces and six pairs of round eyes were turned toward me. They were all obviously wondering how I would handle the situation. I was wondering that myself.

"Well," I said at last, "has anybody seen Carol's earrings?" Everyone shook their heads.

I glanced quickly around the bunkhouse. "Okay, let's pull out the bed and look behind it," I suggested. "They've probably fallen onto the floor."

But they hadn't, and they weren't under the bed, either. If Carol had left them on the windowsill as she claimed, it was very possible that somebody *had* taken them. That meant that we could have a thief in our midst.

"Okay," I said, as cheerfully as I could. I glanced at my watch. "It's time for us to go on the hike. While we're gone, I want everybody to think about where Carol's earrings might be. If any of you has even a *glimmer* of an idea about what might have happened to

them, write it down on a piece of paper." I
went over to my cot, got the box my sunscreen had come in, and placed it on the
windowsill. "All you have to do is fold up the
paper—you don't have to sign your name—
and drop it in here. Before we go to bed
tonight, we'll look in the box and see if there's
anything in it."

"Maybe whoever took my earrings will be
sorry she did it and tell us where she put
them," Carol said hopefully.

"Or maybe somebody will remember a clue,"
Cynthia spoke up, an excited gleam in her
eyes. "I mean, maybe somebody knows something that will reveal where the earrings are.
Like in a Nancy Drew mystery."

"Yeah," Hallie said with interest. "If we had
one clue, we could all be detectives. Hey, that
would be *fun*!"

Carol shook her head. "I don't care about
being a detective. I just want my earrings
back," she said mournfully. "My mother's
going to *kill* me. She didn't want me to bring
them in the first place."

"I have a feeling you'll get them back,"
Cynthia said. She looked around the group.
"Everybody start thinking about clues," she
added in a take-charge tone. "If you think

of *anything*, write it down, no matter how silly you think it is!"

I remembered what Joan had said about letting Cynthia take charge of some activities. It seemed to be working perfectly. The girls were chattering away about the "mystery," Carol was looking hopeful, and Cynthia was busy laying the groundwork for an exciting clue-hunt. I sighed. At least everybody seemed a lot happier. I might have made a mess of things with Dean, but maybe I was turning out to be a good counselor after all!

Chapter Seven

During the next few hours, the girls' excitement over the mystery of Carol's earrings was replaced by their excitement over the hike. It would be our first one, about three miles around the lake.

The trail led out of camp and rose over a rocky embankment. Then it leveled off and curved up above the beach. Pete had told us that the shore below was mostly flat and that we should look for deer and raccoon tracks as well as rabbits and squirrels in the underbrush. Everybody carried a pad and pencil to keep track of interesting things to report on at assembly that night. The counselors were supposed to call the kids' attention to anything unusual. That was a laugh, I thought.

The rocks and trees and ferns were just as unusual to me as they were to the kids. I hardly knew where to begin, so for the first few minutes, I didn't say anything. Nobody else did, either. They were all too breathless from climbing up the embankment.

Suzie was the first to break the silence. "Three miles?" she puffed in discouragement, trudging along behind me. "I'll never make it."

"You'd better make it," Hallie chirped. She still looked fresh and energetic. "If you don't, Pete won't let you go on the all-day hike at the end of the week."

Suzie groaned.

"Is there a bathroom out here?" asked Ginger.

Cynthia glanced at her scornfully. "Bathrooms! Is that all you think about?"

Ginger glanced uneasily into the shadowy pines. "The woods make me nervous. Do you suppose there are bears in there?"

"Don't be silly," I said. I stopped to point at a red and purple spongy thing that was stuck to the roots of a tree. "Oh, look! A mushroom! Isn't it pretty?"

"I bet it'd be good to eat," Suzie said, staring at it hopefully. "We have mushrooms a lot back home. My mother stuffs them with shrimp."

"I bet it's poisonous," Cynthia said loudly for Suzie's benefit.

Ginger backed away. "Poisonous?" She stuck her hands in her pockets.

"Not to touch, silly," Mandy said, squatting beside the mushroom and poking it with her finger. "To eat. Mushrooms can kill you, but first they make you throw up and—"

"Maybe we should make a note of this unusual mushroom for our reports tonight," I interrupted. "We could all draw pictures of it." Dutifully the girls sat down among the ferns and green leaves and reached for their pencils.

"How do you spell mushroom?" Linda wanted to know. "I have to put a label on my picture,"

As Cynthia was spelling it for her, Dean came up the trail, wearing a pack on his back. He stood for a minute staring at us. I swallowed nervously. If Dean had to come along, I was glad he'd happened by in time to see what a good job I was doing as a counselor. Maybe it would help revise the terrible opinion I knew he had of me.

"We're having a nature lesson," I told him, pointing at the mushroom. "We know it's poisonous," I added.

"Oh, yeah?" he asked, the corner of his mouth twitching. "Well, maybe you'd better consider some *other* poisonous elements. As a matter of fact," he added, barely suppressing a grin, "that's poison ivy you're sitting in."

"Poison ivy?" Mandy jumped up and began to scrub her hands on her jeans. "Oh, no! I'm allergic!"

My heart sank like a rock in water. I'd done it *again!* My face flamed.

Dean poked a stick at a three-leaved plant. "You'd better learn to recognize this stuff," he told the girls. "There's a lot of poison ivy in this part of the country."

I looked around helplessly. "What do we do now?"

"Everybody washes," Dean said with a grin, starting up the trail. "There's a brook up the hill. Come on."

With a shake of my head, I followed. I might have known something like this would happen—and that *Dean* would be the one to come along and point it out. I stared at his back. He was probably adding it up right now in his head: city girl plus wilderness camp plus animals plus poison ivy equals trouble. I sighed wearily. Add that to the fact that I'd pulled my hand away from him just when he was trying to be romantic, and what do you get? Disaster, that's what.

It only took a few minutes to get to the little brook, which was babbling contentedly over the rocks as it made its way down to the lake. Under Dean's direction, we all scrubbed our legs and arms with a scrap of soap he fished out of his pack, and then we set off again. The rest of the hike, blessedly, was uneventful. We caught a glimpse of three deer—a doe with two fawns—and we found some raccoon tracks beside the trail. Cynthia swore she heard a moose crashing through the woods. We wrote everything down for our reports, and Hallie took a picture of the raccoon tracks for her scrapbook. By the time we got back to the bunkhouse, everybody's feet hurt and Mandy was already beginning to itch.

I went off to ask Joan for some calamine lotion. When I got back, Cynthia was holding up the box I'd left on the windowsill. "Hey, look!" she said. "There's a piece of paper in there!"

"My earrings!" Carol exclaimed. "Maybe somebody's found them!"

"That's funny," Hallie remarked. "I looked in the box a minute ago, and it was empty."

I handed the calamine lotion to Mandy and went over to Cynthia. I hadn't really expected the box strategy to yield anything. "You mean, there's really something *in* it?" I asked, surprised. "Let's see."

Cynthia handed me the box. "*You* open it," she instructed.

The girls all gathered around as I opened the box and pulled out a piece of white paper that had been folded into a tiny square. There was something printed on it in scrawling, childish-looking letters. "If you're looking for a clue to this mystery," I read aloud, "don't give up. It's in the bag."

"In the bag?" Carol repeated blankly. "Somebody put my earrings in a *bag*? Who would want to do that?"

"Somebody's playing a game," I said accusingly, looking around. "Okay, which one of you is it?"

Six innocent faces gazed up at me. "A game?" Mandy asked. She opened the calamine bottle and sniffed it, wrinkling her nose. "Who would want to play a game with Carol's earrings?"

"It's a *scavenger* hunt!" Linda said excitedly. "Like at a birthday party!"

"I think it's a *lousy* game, if you ask me,"

Carol said angrily. "Whoever's got my ear-rings had better give them back right this minute, or there's going to be trouble."

"It's in the bag," Cynthia mused. She scratched her head, her eyes sparkling. "Which bag, do you suppose?"

"The garbage bag?" Hallie suggested. We all trooped over to the wastebasket in the corner and pulled its plastic liner out, but it was empty.

Just then the supper bell rang.

"I guess our mystery will have to wait," I said. "It's time for supper."

"Yeah," Suzie said, brightening. "And we're having pizza!"

"I don't see how you can be hungry," Ginger piped up, "when you've been eating choco-late-chip cookies ever since we got back from the hike."

"But I *had* to," Suzie protested. "All that walking made me hungry."

I frowned at Suzie. "Hey, what about Pete's rule? We're not supposed to have food in the bunkhouse, remember?"

"I guess I forgot," Suzie said guiltily, study-ing her sneakers.

"Will you promise to get rid of any cookies that are left?"

With a sigh, Suzie nodded. "I promise," she said. "Do you suppose it'll be *thick*-crust pizza?" she added eagerly.

"So how's the poison ivy victim?" Dean asked. He put his plate down on the table and climbed over the bench to sit down beside me.

"She's a little itchy," I said. "But she says it's usually worse by now, so maybe it won't be too bad. I guess I should have been more careful."

I glanced at him out of the corner of my eye. It was the first time I'd seen him without his battered brown hat, and if anything, he was even better-looking. It was also the first time he'd made an effort to sit with me at a meal. My stomach felt the way it does when I go up in an elevator too fast, and I wondered whether I'd be able to manage my supper.

Dean shrugged. "Listen, Tabby, don't take it to heart—about the poison ivy, I mean. I've lived around the stuff all my life, and I still manage to get a good dose of it every now and then." He picked up his pizza and took a bite. "Other than the poison ivy, how's it going in your bunkhouse?"

I laughed, encouraged that he was acting

as if he didn't think I was a *total* fool. "It depends on who you ask, I guess. Suzie's happy because she's got a supply of chocolate-chip cookies under her bed. Carol's unhappy because she's sure somebody took her earrings. But on the other hand, Cynthia's happy because she's out to solve the mystery of the missing earrings. And somebody's leaving clues for us to find them, like a scavenger hunt. Tonight's clue is 'It's in the bag.' "

Dean grinned. "I'm not sure I understand all of that," he said, "but it sounds as if you're off to a flying start."

"Well, it's a start, anyway," I admitted, feeling better and better. "I don't know about the flying part."

Dean grinned. "Just hang in there," he said encouragingly, putting his arm around me and giving me a hug. "It'll be all right."

All right? I thought, feeling the warmth of his arm across my shoulders. It was absolute heaven! But just at that moment, Joan and Mother came through the door with trays full of pizzas. Mother looked straight at me, and both her eyebrows went up in that quizzical way that always means "What's going on here? What are you up to now?" Then she gave me a mischievous grin.

I looked down at my plate. Then, not knowing what else to do, I leaned forward abruptly so that Dean's arm sort of slid off my shoulders. At the same time, I began to cough—an artificial-sounding cough, but the best I could manage on the spur of the moment. Dean began to pound me on the back.

"Are you okay?" he asked.

I nodded. My face was red, and there were tears in my eyes—but not from coughing. I was feeling lower than I'd ever felt in my life. Just when it looked as if our relationship might be taking a new turn, I had messed it up again.

"Hi, everybody!" It was Randy and Heidi.

Randy sat down on the other side of the table with his plate full of pizza, and Heidi sat beside him. She smiled at me across the table, and I smiled back, grateful for the interruption. Anyway, since the water-bucket episode, I'd come to like Heidi. I had the feeling that if we had more time to spend together, we could become good friends.

"You know what I think?" Randy asked, taking a huge bite of his pizza. As usual, he didn't wait for an answer. "I think that Marge should make pizza every night. Why don't we take a vote on it?"

At that moment Mother came over to our table with Joan right behind her. Their arms were loaded with trays full of pizza slices.

"Seconds, anybody?" Mother asked. Tonight she had her dark hair pulled back into a ponytail like mine. In her jeans and Camp Cherokee T-shirt, she looked almost like a teenager. In fact, if you didn't know the truth, you probably wouldn't believe that she was my mother.

"Over here!" Randy waved both arms over his head. "Seconds and thirds."

"Ditto that," Dean said.

"I'm glad you like it," Mother said, putting a whole tray down in front of us.

Randy looked up at Mother. "It's great!" Then he glanced over at me and frowned. "You know," he said thoughtfully, "there's something about you and Tabby that—"

I gulped. Oh, no! In another instant, Randy was going to *guess*! "Dean," I interrupted hastily in a squeaky voice, "do you want another slice of pizza?"

Mother turned to go back into the kitchen, but Randy kept right on staring at me. I could feel my ears beginning to turn pink. "I can't quite put my finger on it, but—" he began.

91

"Thanks," Dean told me, his mouth full. "In a minute, okay?"

Randy shook his head. "You know, it's really weird, but I'd swear—"

I was desperate. I *had* to turn the conversation in a different direction. I leaned toward Heidi. "You know," I babbled brightly, "the most awful thing happened today. In my bunkhouse, I mean."

Heidi gave me an odd look. "Oh yeah? What?"

"Somebody stole some valuable earrings from one of the girls."

"Hey, that *is* awful," Heidi said, her expression serious. "Have you reported it to Pete?"

"Not yet. Do you think I ought to?"

"Sure," Heidi said. "Don't you, Dean?"

He nodded. "That would be a good idea, I guess."

"The thing is," I continued, with a quick glance at Randy, "that whoever took them is leaving us clues." Maybe I could breathe a little easier now. Randy was thoroughly occupied with his pizza, and he seemed to have forgotten what he was going to say about Marge and me. "Like in a scavenger hunt," I added. "The first clue was 'It's in the bag,' whatever that means. I'm beginning to wonder whether the thief isn't more interested in the game than the earrings. If that's the case, it probably wouldn't hurt to play along with it for a while."

I relaxed a bit. It seemed as if the danger was past.

Then Mother came back with another load of pizza for the next table, and Randy looked up.

Suddenly a wide grin spread across his face. "I've got it!" he exclaimed triumphantly.

"Got what?" Dean asked, frowning.

"Look at them! They look just alike!"

I thought I was going to be sick. I swallowed hard.

"*Who* looks alike?" Heidi demanded.

"Why, Marge and Tabby!" Randy said. "They could be *sisters*." He peered at me. "I'll bet they *are* sisters. Or cousins, at least. Hey, isn't that right, Tabby? How come you didn't tell us?"

The room began to spin. Now I *really* felt sick.

Chapter Eight

With a giggle, Mother looked across the table at me. By this time the whole dining hall had heard Randy, and they were all staring at us.

I put a hand over my eyes. I could tell that my face was already crimson. It was all over now. Concealing the fact that Marge was my mother was bad enough, but to pretend I didn't know her?

"No, Randy," I said finally, "we're not sisters. Marge is my"—I gulped—"mother."

"Your mother?" Heidi yelped.

"But she looks like your *sister*," Randy said unbelievingly. "I mean, she can't possibly be old enough . . ." He stopped, embarrassed for once in his life.

"Just for that, Randy," my mother told him, "you've earned an extra helping of dessert." Laughing, she went back into the kitchen, leaving me to cope with this mess all by myself.

Dean was staring at me. "Marge is your mother? Then why did you act like you didn't know one another on the first day of camp? And how come you took the bus instead of driving with her?"

It was the worst moment of my life. I felt like a worm.

"Because . . ." I began unhappily, and then stopped. Why *had* I done it? Why had it seemed important to pretend I'd come to Camp Cherokee by myself? Suddenly the reasons that had made so much sense a week before seemed childish and silly.

"Because why?" he asked, looking bewildered. He was probably thinking that a normal person wouldn't disown her own mother. Now he'd never be interested in me as anything more than a friend. And I couldn't blame him.

"Listen," Heidi said tactfully, "Randy and I have something important we have to ask Pete." She stood up. "Don't we, Randy?"

"We do?" Randy asked, surprised. "But I haven't finished my pizza yet. And Marge said I could have seconds on dessert."

"Then bring your precious food along," Heidi said firmly. "We can have dessert over at Pete's table."

"But—"

"Bring it along," Heidi repeated with a meaningful glance, and after a second Randy got up, too.

Suddenly everyone else got up and left, too, leaving Dean and me alone together at the table. I wasn't sure whether I should be glad that I didn't have to face Randy's teasing, or whether to wish they were still there so I wouldn't have to face Dean all by myself. But now I didn't have any choice.

"Okay," Dean said finally. "Are you going to tell me, or are you just going to let this stay a big mystery?"

I cleared my throat. "Well," I said miserably, "there's not a lot to tell, actually." I picked up my fork and began to make little dents in the edge of my Styrofoam plate. The minute I told him the story, I knew our semi-relationship would be over permanently. I might as well tell him the truth. It couldn't possibly make things worse than they were already, and at least then the air would be cleared.

"Well, for starters," I began slowly, "Pete is my uncle. He's my mother's brother."

"Oh," Dean said. "So that's how he found you."

"Yeah," I said. "I was all set to go to sailing camp with a friend of mine when Pete called. He needed a cook and a counselor, and he sounded really desperate. I . . . I didn't want to come at all because I'd made these other plans, but—"

"But you couldn't really get out of it because it was a family thing," Dean finished for me.

I threw him a grateful look. "Right. I mean, I really *like* Pete and Joan"—it sounded funny now to say Uncle and Aunt—"and I wanted them to make a go of this camp, so I agreed to come. But I—I didn't want it to look like I had to have my mother tagging along, like she was supervising me or something. It was just too embarrassing, that's all."

I stopped. Now that I was trying to put my logic into words, I could see just how stupid it had been. My mother wasn't the sort of parent who felt she had to keep checking up on me all the time. She trusted me.

"So you decided not to tell anyone that she was your mother," Dean prompted.

I nodded mutely and began to punch little holes in the middle of my plate with my fork.

"Yeah." I swallowed. "It was sort of a dumb idea, I guess."

There was a long silence, and then Dean said, "Well, not really, Tab."

I turned to look at him. He was carefully pleating his paper napkin into some sort of fan.

"It's not dumb to want to be on your own," he said finally, concentrating on his napkin.

"You really think so?" The skin on my arms was beginning to prickle.

Dean nodded. He folded the fan again, and all of a sudden it was a bird, one of those paper cranes the Japanese believe are good luck. "Yeah," he replied, looking up. "That's what Cherokee is all about, isn't it? Kids getting a chance to be independent, I mean." His brown eyes held mine, and my stomach started its elevator trips up and down again.

"Maybe it was kind of silly to pretend that your mother wasn't your mother," Dean continued. "But I understand how you felt." He grinned wryly. "In fact, something like that happened to me, too."

I let out my breath. I hadn't even realized I'd been holding it. "Really?" I asked.

"Until last year, my older brother Sam was the senior counselor here. I *hated* the fact that everyone knew I was Sam's kid brother. If there'd been any way to pretend that I was somebody else, I would have done it in a flash."

I couldn't believe it. Here was practically perfect Dean, confessing that he'd wanted to play the same kind of silly trick I'd played.

Dean chuckled. "I was really glad when Sam got a job doing construction this summer." He looked at me. "See what I mean?"

I nodded. Maybe—just maybe—there was a glimmer of hope for us. I felt almost giddy with the thought of it.

He was still looking at me, turning the white paper bird in his fingers. Then he reached for my hand and put the bird into it very gently, as if he were putting it in a nest. "Here," he said. His eyes remained fastened on mine, and the room seemed to fade into the background, leaving just us there together. "For good luck."

Then Dean picked up his hat, climbed over the bench, and walked away.

"Hey, what are you doing going through my duffel bag?" It was Hallie, and she was glaring at Ginger.

"The clue said the earrings were 'in the

99

bag.' " Ginger said defensively. "I saw your bag on your bed and I thought it might be the right one."

"Well, it isn't," Hallie snapped. She turned to me. "Tabby, tell Ginger to stay out of my stuff."

I leaned my guitar against the wall beside my cot. It was almost nine o'clock, and the girls were getting ready for bed. They sounded tired and cross. But I was still feeling sort of floaty after my talk with Dean, floaty and wonderful. I put Dean's bird on my pillow and smiled at Ginger. "Ginger, don't bother other people's things, okay?"

" 'It's in the bag,' " Cynthia mused from her bed. "What do you suppose—?" Suddenly she jumped up. "I've got it!" she shouted, snapping her fingers. She rushed for the white cotton laundry bag, hanging half-full on the wall.

"Oh, I don't think—" I began.

"Here it is!" Cynthia crowed. "I *told* you so!"

"My earrings?" Carol screamed, jumping out of bed. "You've found them?"

"Well, one of them, anyway," Cynthia told her. "But it looks like there's another clue. Here, Tabby. You read it."

I walked over to the light and opened the folded scrap of paper Cynthia had handed me. "To find the other earring, go look where you see yourself," I read slowly, squinting to decipher the childish print. "And then look where you aren't."

"Another clue!" Suzie jumped up and down and clapped her hands. "Just like a scavenger hunt!"

Carol stamped her foot, pouting. "I don't *care* about clues—I want my earring back!"

"Go look where you see yourself," Linda repeated slowly. "And then look where you aren't. Where do you suppose *that* place is?"

"I don't know," I replied, looking at my watch, "but there's one place we have to go right now."

"Where's that?" the girls chorused.

"To bed," I said firmly. "It's time for lights-out."

It took the girls quite a while to settle down. I could hear them rustling and giggling for twenty minutes at least, whispering about the new clue and trying to figure out what it could possibly mean. Then I had to get my flashlight and take Ginger down the path to the bathroom.

But at last Ginger was in bed and there

was silence, except for Merlin's eerie *whoo-whoo* from outside and the soft sound of Suzie's snoring. Everyone was finally asleep.

Except me.

It wasn't the clue that was keeping me awake. I kept thinking of Dean, and the way his eyes had held mine. It *had* really happened, hadn't it? Yes, there was the paper bird, proof that it hadn't been a dream. He must like me, I told myself. But I knew I shouldn't make too much of things. He'd put the bird into my hand, that was all—he hadn't really *held* it. But I kept on imagining and imagining. By the time I'd started drifting off to sleep, I could almost feel the light touch of Dean's lips on mine and the quick brush of his fingers across my cheek.

Scritch, scritch, scritch.

My imagination shut itself off with a snap, and I sat bolt upright. Something was inside the bunkhouse!

Scritch-scritch. The noise was louder this time. I reached for my flashlight, my heart pounding. In the next bed, Ginger stirred and whimpered, and then she sat up, too.

"What is it?" she asked, pulling the sheet up under her chin. "What's that awful noise? Is it a bear?"

"A bear?" Hallie asked sleepily. "Did somebody say there was a *bear* in here?"

"Don't be silly," I said firmly. "There are no bears around here." I *hope*, I added to myself, much more tentatively. My heart skipped a couple more beats.

SCRITCH-SCRITCH. Whatever it was, it was certainly making a *lot* of noise.

"Hey, it's over here," Mandy said from the corner. Her voice was a fearful, muffled whisper. "It's right *beside* me!"

We all listened a moment. The scratching had stopped, and the only sound was Suzie's gentle snoring. Then the scratching started again, more energetically, and we heard the sound of paper tearing. It was obviously time to act.

"What are you going to do, Tabby?" Linda asked tremulously. "Do you have a gun?"

What *was* I going to do? All I had was my flashlight, and my cowardice about animals. I was sure that good camp counselors weren't cowards. Taking a deep breath, I swung my legs out of bed and padded barefoot down the middle aisle, following the sound to the back corner of the bunkhouse, between Mandy's and Suzie's cots.

"Stay in your beds," I commanded everyone

in an authoritative whisper, hoping the girls wouldn't notice that my voice was shaking. "Don't anybody get up."

"Are you kidding?" Cynthia whispered back, cowering under her blanket. "You wouldn't catch *me* walking around barefoot with a wild animal loose in here."

"Yeah," Ginger added. "Especially if it's a bear."

I flashed my light around the back wall. Nothing. But the sound was definitely louder, and coming from underneath Suzie's bed. Cautiously, trying to assure myself that there was absolutely nothing to fear from an animal that could fit under a bed, I squatted to lift up one corner of Suzie's blanket. As I shone my light under the bed, I could see twin red gleams—eyes!

"Shoo!" I cried, waving my flashlight like a stick. "Go on! Scat! Get out of here! Go home!"

"Sschumpht?" Suzie asked, still asleep. She turned over heavily, and under her bed the two eyes blinked. I swallowed. My mouth suddenly felt as if it were full of sawdust.

"Here," Mandy called from the bed in the corner. She leaned over to hand me a tennis shoe. "Throw this at it."

I did. There was a solid THUMP and a

squeak, and the red eyes blinked again, but the creature didn't move. Suzie rolled over the other way.

"Try the other shoe," Mandy urged, handing it to me. "But throw it harder this time."

THUMP! That did it. There was a loud, indignant squawk, and the animal backed out from under Suzie's bed, dragging something in its teeth. At that moment one of the girls turned on the lights.

"A skunk!" Mandy shouted, leaping up onto her bed.

"A skunk?" Cynthia screeched in a panic. "Let me out of here!" She immediately dashed for the door, with the rest of the girls—except for Suzie, who was miraculously still asleep—hard on her heels.

And, oblivious to all of the chaos, Lilac hunched down happily with the giant Hershey bar he had dragged out from under Suzie's bed.

Chapter Nine

By the time I'd gotten to the part about the Hershey bar, Heidi was doubled over, laughing. It was late afternoon the next day, and the two of us were out on a raft, thirty yards offshore, keeping an eye on the kids in the water.

"So it was just Lilac," Heidi gasped, "raiding the pantry."

I nodded. "Suzie promised to get rid of her chocolate-chip cookies after Ginger squealed on her yesterday afternoon. But she didn't think anybody knew about her candy." I giggled. "It turned out that she had quite a stash under her bed—Hershey bars, licorice whips, gummy bears, you name it. After I shooed Lilac out of the bunkhouse and the girls came back in, we woke Suzie up and badgered her into sharing her goodies with all of us. We had a terrific midnight feast. The candy's completely gone now."

"That's good." Heidi stuck her whistle in her mouth and blew a sharp blast at a boy who had just ducked his swimming buddy for the third time. "Lilac's a *fiend* for anything sweet, especially chocolate. He's even been known to chew his way through the screen on the kitchen door looking for dessert."

"I didn't know skunks liked people food," I said. "I thought they ate mostly roots and berries and stuff."

"They do," Heidi said, "when they're raised in the wild. But Lilac was orphaned a couple of years ago, and Sam, Dean's older brother, gave him scraps from the dining hall." She looked at me. "Did Dean tell you about Sam? He was a counselor here until last year."

"Yes," I said, "he did." I adjusted the strap of my new black swimsuit. I'd been so sure that Mother would object to its not having any back to speak of, but she'd just grinned when she saw me wearing it this morning and told me I was getting a good tan.

Heidi pulled off her red sun visor and tossed it down beside her. She didn't need it. The sun hadn't shone all afternoon. "Listen," she said, "I hope you're not too mad at Randy about last night at supper. Sometimes he's a real turkey about teasing, but underneath he's a nice guy."

I blushed. "I ought to apologize, too. About trying to fool everybody, I mean. I guess I didn't think the whole thing through." I looked up. "Hey, Ralph," I yelled to one of Dean's campers, "enough splashing, okay?"

Heidi waved a hand. "Forget it, Tabby. It's no big deal." She gave me a curious look. "Listen, if I'm not being nosy, how are you and Dean getting along?"

"You're not being nosy," I said. It felt good to have somebody to talk girl-talk with, the way I did with Megan. "I just wish"—I knew I was blushing again—"I could be sure he really likes me, that's all. After all the stuff with my mother and the animals and . . ." My voice trailed off.

Heidi shook her head. "He likes you," she said. "A lot."

"He does?" I asked breathlessly. "How do you know?"

She smiled wisely. "Because he told Randy so last night."

"He did?" I was astonished.

Heidi laughed and nodded. "He told Randy he thinks you've been a good sport about everything. And he thinks you're really pretty." Suddenly she jumped up again and blew her whistle at a kid standing on the edge of the raft. "Hey, Chuck," she yelled. "If you're going to jump in backwards, you'd better have eyes in the back of your head!"

I shut my eyes briefly. Dean thought I was pretty! He thought I was *really* pretty! I opened my eyes again. All of a sudden the afternoon sun came out, brushing the lake's ripples with gold, and the golden rays touched my arm and shoulder, making them warm. I was glowing inside, too. He thought I was pretty!

Heidi turned back to me. "So what about the missing earrings?" she asked. "Have you and your kids solved the big mystery yet?"

"Well, we've solved half of it, I guess," I replied. Turning my thoughts away from Dean was an immense effort. I told Heidi about Cynthia's finding one of the earrings in the laundry bag, and about the second clue.

"Go look where you see yourself," she mused. "Hmm. Sounds like a mirror, doesn't it?"

I nodded. "I looked at the one in the bathroom this morning, but I didn't find anything. It's the second part of the clue that's got me stumped. One of those girls has a really good imagination, or else she's been reading too many mystery stories."

"Look where you aren't." Heidi put her visor back on and pushed her blond bangs out of her eyes. "It might be the back side of the mirror. Hey, I'll bet I know where it is, Tabby." She glanced at her watch. "We've got to get going, anyway. It's almost time for supper." She stood up and blew her whistle. "Okay, everybody out!" she called loudly.

"But I told you, Heidi," I said, as we stood in the girls' bathroom a few minutes later. "I've already looked all around the mirror. I even tried to take it off the wall to look behind it, but it's been up there so long that the screws are rusted tight." I shook my head. "There must be another mirror in this camp somewhere."

Heidi smiled. "Come on," she said. "We're going behind the mirror, like Alice in *Through the Looking-Glass*." She opened a door in the wall.

"What is this place?" I asked as Heidi switched on a bare overhead bulb.

"A broom closet," she replied, running her fingers along a ledge on the wall right behind the mirror. "Ah-ha!" she exclaimed. "Is *this* what we're looking for?" In her hand was Carol's second turquoise earring.

"That's it!" I cried, delighted. "The mystery's solved! Thanks, Heidi."

Heidi handed the earring to me. "Yeah—*one* mystery, anyway."

"What do you mean?" I asked.

Heidi shrugged. "Well, we still don't know who took the earrings in the first place." She frowned. "One of the kids in your bunkhouse obviously has a problem."

I thought of Suzie's weight problem and Ginger's thumb-sucking problem and Cynthia's bossiness problem. There were plenty of others, too. "Take your pick," I said with a sigh.

It was early the next morning, and Pete had gathered the counselors together to go over plans for the canoe trip we were going to take that day. I'd been looking forward to it with a sort of nervous anticipation. I hoped fervently that paddling a canoe was one of those skills that you never forgot, like riding a bicycle or doing the butterfly. I didn't want to disgrace myself in front of Dean and everybody else because I couldn't steer straight.

111

"Each canoe holds ten people," Pete was saying, "so there should be plenty of room for everybody, including Marge, who's coming along with our lunch—that is, if nobody minds." He winked at me, and I blushed.

"As long as she doesn't bring alfalfa sandwiches again," Randy grumbled.

"Randy," Heidi said disgustedly. "*Really.*"

Dean grinned and tipped his hat to me. I gave him a quick smile and then looked away. Ever since Heidi had told me that he thought I was pretty, I'd felt shy about meeting his eyes directly.

"I was in the kitchen a few minutes ago," Dean told Randy, "and Marge said we're having chicken salad sandwiches. And chocolate cookies."

"All *right*," Randy said enthusiastically. I snickered quietly. I knew about those chocolate cookies.

"It'd probably be better if each counselor takes the kids from his or her own bunkhouse," Pete went on. "That way we won't mix age-groups and the younger kids won't feel outclassed. Be sure you take enough paddles, and don't forget life jackets. We'll leave the dock at nine-thirty. You can take your time getting across the lake—stop at the marsh, if you want to, and look for red-winged blackbird nests, or pull in under the willows. There's a muskrat den there, and if your kids are real quiet, they might see the little musk-rats." He looked around at our group. "Any questions?"

I bit my lip and glanced at Randy, remembering what he'd said about alligators. Had he been teasing? I really didn't want to ask, but I couldn't afford not to know. "Uh, Pete," I said, putting up my hand tentatively. "What about alligators?"

"Alligators?" Pete asked, looking puzzled.

Randy snickered. "Oh, you know," he said. "The ones that crawled up here from Louisiana after the Civil War and—"

Pete laughed loudly. "I don't think you've got anything to worry about, Tabby. Nobody but Randy has ever seen those alligators." My face burned. I should have known that it was just a joke.

Randy looked injured. "Listen, if nobody else has ever seen them, it's because nobody ever *looks*. I'll bet if we offered a prize to everybody who spotted one, we'd have lots of sightings."

The meeting broke up with a laugh.

"How about hanging around together this

morning?" Dean asked me as we left the room. "I can show your kids the muskrat den, if you want."

"That would be nice," I said, still feeling a bit shy. I mustered enough courage to steal a glance at him from the corner of my eye. He was smiling, and his smile made my heart do a flip-flop. "I'm sure the girls would really like that. I would, too," I added.

"Okay," he said casually. He touched my arm lightly. "See you at the dock."

I watched him walk away. Had we just made a date? I wondered. But then I pulled myself up short. Maybe he was just worried about whether I could safely handle a canoe with seven kids in it. And even if it *was* a date, we weren't likely to have much privacy. Not with fourteen chaperons looking on.

"I don't *care* if it's a game!" Hallie was saying angrily when I got back to the bunkhouse. "I want my locket back. Right *now*!"

"Okay," Cynthia said in a commanding tone, looking around at the rest of the girls. "Who took Hallie's locket?"

I frowned. "Has there been another theft?"

Hallie jumped up. "Somebody took my gold locket out of my duffel bag," she said. She

114

turned to Ginger. "I'll bet it was *you*," she accused her. "You were the one who was messing around in my bag before. Where did you put it?"

Ginger's face screwed up. "I *didn't*," she wailed tearfully. "It wasn't me. Honest, Hallie."

"Well, then, who?" Hallie asked, whirling around.

"Were there any clues?" Cynthia asked. "Did the villain leave any evidence at the scene of the crime?"

"You and your clues," Carol said, sounding disgusted. She put her arm around Hallie. "It's okay, Hallie. We'll get your locket back."

"Not without clues, we won't," Cynthia put in gleefully.

I sighed. "Listen, everybody, it's time for our canoe trip," I said. "We can hunt for clues later." I turned to Hallie. "I'm sure your locket will turn up, Hallie. After all, we got Carol's earrings back, didn't we? Somebody must be playing a game, that's all."

"Well, it's a stupid game," Hallie grumbled. "Somebody in this bunkhouse sure has a weird sense of humor."

I had to agree.

Chapter Ten

The morning passed pleasantly. The canoe was a big one, a good six feet longer than the one I'd learned on at scout camp, but Dean showed me some tricks with the paddle and pretty soon I could steer almost as straight as he could.

None of the girls had ever been in a canoe before, much less held a paddle, but they were having enormous fun. Cynthia was sitting in the bow of the canoe, pretending that she was Christopher Columbus sighting the New World. Linda was keeping a running tally on the number of turtles she spotted napping on floating logs. Even Hallie seemed to have forgotten about her missing locket as she gleefully pointed out a green leopard frog sitting on a lily pad, waiting for his lunch to happen along. When we got to the muskrat den, Dean made us all be very quiet and then pointed out two tiny brown noses poking out of a hole in the bank. The girls were elated, and even Dean's boys seemed impressed.

When the sun was high in the sky, we headed toward the opposite shore and lunch. There was a picnic table in a clearing among the pines. Neither of the other canoes had arrived yet.

"Race you to the shore," Dean called over to us. It wasn't exactly a fair race, since Dean's boys were older and stronger than my girls. But Dean seemed to be dragging his paddle in the water, which sort of evened things out until we got close to shore. By the time we were half a football field from the rocky beach, though, Dean started to paddle, too, and the boys began to outdistance us easily.

"Hey, they're winning!" Cynthia shouted from the bow. "Paddle faster!"

"We're paddling as fast as we can," Hallie yelled back. "*You* paddle faster!"

"Ooh, look!" Mandy pointed with her paddle to a large V-shaped ripple in the water a few feet away from the canoe. I looked twice to be sure it wasn't one of Randy's imaginary alligators, but I was pretty sure it wasn't.

"It's a snake!" Linda cried. "A *big* one, too! Isn't it a snake, Tabby? What kind is it? Will it bite?"

"A snake?" Suzie shrieked, snatching her paddle out of the water. "Don't let it come near me! I *hate* snakes!" She stood up suddenly, holding her paddle as if to defend herself from the invading monster.

"Suzie, sit down!" I commanded as the canoe teetered dangerously. "You'll capsize us!"

"A snake?" Ginger asked with interest. "Where?" She got up, too.

"Hey!" I shouted. "Everybody *down*, or we'll—"

"Yiiiiiikes!" Cynthia cried. "We're tipping!"

It was too late. As Ginger leaned to look for the snake, the canoe tipped to one side. Suzie flailed madly to keep her balance, and Ginger grabbed a handful of Hallie's hair, trying to hold on. But it was no use. In an instant we were all in the water.

"Help!" Suzie shrieked frantically. "I can't swim! I'm drowning!" And I saw to my horror that her life jacket, which she'd apparently unzipped, had come off and was floating away!

"Stay calm, everybody," I yelled, treading water. "Hang on to the canoe, if you can." The shore wasn't that far away, only about twenty yards, and everybody but Suzie seemed to have life jackets on. None of the girls were very experienced swimmers, but I figured they wouldn't be in any real danger unless they panicked. I swam quickly toward Suzie, who was going down again.

By this time Dean's canoe had reached the shore and the boys were scattering to explore the woods. But when Dean looked back and saw what was happening, he pulled off his hat and jumped into the water.

"Hang on, Tabby!" he shouted reassuringly. "I'll give you a hand." He began to swim out toward us with strong, swift strokes.

It took a few minutes, but I was finally able to haul Suzie, scared and sputtering, to shore. Dean had already pulled in Cynthia and Mandy. Then I swam out to help Linda and Ginger, who were still clinging to the upside-down canoe. We kicked and splashed and managed to push it into shore while Dean gave Carol a hand. Hallie made it on her own.

"Is everybody in?" Dean asked, as we stood

dripping on the bank. My wet T-shirt was stuck to me, my knees were smeared with mud, and there was a strand of smelly green lake weed hanging off my nose, but this wasn't the time to worry about how I looked.

"All present and accounted for," I said, quickly counting heads. I glanced at Suzie, who was sitting on a rock sniffling. "Are you okay, Suzie?"

"I almost drowned," she whimpered, looking up at me with big round eyes. "I *would* have drowned if you hadn't pulled me in. You were so brave, Tabby."

I shrugged. "I didn't—"

Dean stopped me with a look. "That was a super job you did out there," he said quietly. He stepped closer and put both hands on my arms, his eyes intent on mine. "If you'd lost your head, it could have been a real disaster. I'm really proud of you."

Who was I to argue? After everything that had happened since I'd come to Camp Cherokee, I wasn't about to turn down a compliment from Dean. Then he astonished me by pulling me close and kissing me. All I could do was shut my eyes and kiss him back as seven girls jumped up and down, clapping and cheering wildly. I held my breath and hung on while my heart did sensational roller coaster dips and loop-the-loops. It was the most wonderful kiss of my entire life.

Finally Dean dropped his hands and stepped back. "Hey," he said, grinning, "you've got a piece of weed hanging on your nose." He brushed it off gently.

Mandy gave a long sigh. "Wow," she breathed dreamily. "Wasn't that romantic? Just like *All My Children.*"

"I'm *not* going!" Cynthia was sitting on her cot, her arms folded across her chest and a stubborn pout on her face. "I don't care about taking some old hike up a stupid mountain. I'm staying here."

I sat down on the edge of her cot. "Look, Cynthia," I began, "just because your mother called to—"

"It has nothing to do with my mother," Cynthia growled.

Ginger looked up from tying her shoelaces. "Listen, Cynthia, you should come with us. We're taking Lucille, and it'll be a lot of fun. I've never been on a hike with a llama before."

Neither had I, and I wasn't sure it was an experience I wanted. Nevertheless, carrying necessities such as lunch and drinks on all-day hikes was part of Lucille's job, and most of the kids were excited about going. Everyone but Cynthia. She'd been fine until her mother called to see how she was getting along. Now she was in another one of her stormy, stubborn moods.

Hallie came up to me looking worried. "It's been a whole day," she reminded me.

"A whole day since what?" I asked absently, still trying to figure out how to deal with Cynthia.

"Since my locket disappeared," she said unhappily. "You said we'd get it back."

"Well, we haven't gotten it back," Cynthia said with a lofty look, "because there haven't been any clues. How can we do detective work without them?"

Hallie scowled at her. "Well, there'd better be a clue in a hurry," she said darkly, "or—"

Ginger tugged at my arm. "Tabby, does Lucille bite?" she asked worriedly.

I sighed. Sometimes I felt as if I were juggling a half dozen balls in the air, and in about ten seconds I was going to drop all of them.

"No," I replied. "Lucille doesn't bite. But

she might decide to lick you. Don't worry—it just tickles." To Hallie, I said, "Since we haven't found your locket, I think we'd better report it to Pete as stolen. Maybe he'll have an idea about what to do." Then I took a deep breath and turned to Cynthia. "Cynthia," I threatened, "you get off that bed and put your shoes on now, or *else*." It was the first time I had used that tone of voice, which was about as stern as my mother's had ever gotten with me. I wasn't sure it was going to work.

It didn't.

"Or else what?" Cynthia asked, unmoved.

"Or else," Dean said casually from the doorway, "it'll be *your* job to stay here all alone and guard the camp from bears. Marge and Joan are going to town for the day, and everybody else is coming on the hike."

I looked at Dean and then looked away again quickly, feeling enormously awkward. Ever since he'd kissed me the day before, I hadn't thought of much else. I could feel him standing there, and my heart began to pound wildly.

Cynthia looked at me suspiciously. "I thought you said there weren't any bears around here," she said.

"There aren't," Dean replied before I could.

"Not usually, that is. There are too many people, and most bears don't like to come where people are. But the ranger at the fire station just called to report a bear sighting up on the ridge, so we have to be on the lookout." He turned to Cynthia with a grin. "That's why we'd be very happy to leave you here if you want to stay. It'll be your job to guard the camp against any intruders."

Cynthia stared at him for a minute. Then she scrambled off her cot and began to hunt for her shoes. "Changed my mind," she muttered. "Guess I'll go on the hike."

I turned to ask Dean privately about the bear sighting. Was it for real, or was it something he'd made up on the spot to convince Cynthia to come with us? But he'd already started up the path, and soon, in the flurry of making sure that everyone was ready for the hike, I forgot about the matter altogether. We finished putting on our shoes and our mosquito repellent and our sunglasses and finally trooped out to the Assembly Circle to wait for Pete to bring Lucille, her pack loaded with lunch goodies.

It was a great hike. Even I, who had never been much of a hiker, enjoyed following the trail up past Rocky Point, where we could look down over the lake. We paused there for a few minutes while Cynthia pointed out to everyone the exact spot where Suzie had capsized the canoe. The way Cynthia told the story was blood-chilling.

"Wow," Pete said admiringly when she'd finished, "that must have been quite an adventure."

"Just like in the movies," I said with a laugh. "Of course, it didn't all happen exactly the way Cynthia told it, but—"

"It did *so*!" Cynthia insisted indignantly. "Every word was true!"

We all laughed and continued our hike, up to Hawkins Meadow, which was decorated with red and purple wildflowers, drifts of yellow butterflies, and iridescent hummingbirds. We had lunch there, so Dean and I took our sandwiches and sat on a rock at the edge of the little brook that ran through the meadow.

It was the first time we had actually gotten to talk together, and we had to make up for lost time. At first I felt shy, but after a few minutes that wore off, and I was soon talking as easily as Dean. We traded stories about Camp Cherokee and Pete and Joan and Heidi and Randy, and about school and our families and lots else. Dean confided that he hated being the youngest of five brothers and sisters, and I confessed that I was lonely sometimes being an only child. It was a wonderful conversation, but there was one thing wrong. Our talk skirted the most important topic—*us.* I wanted Dean to say something like, "Is there any chance you'll be coming back to Camp Cherokee next summer?" and I was dying to ask, "Do you ever get as far east as Washington?" Instead we stayed with safe topics, which were about everything but us. I didn't know how to introduce the subject without seeming pushy.

Dean was in the middle of telling me about his long-term plans, which included majoring in forestry and becoming a park ranger, when Pete called that it was time to go. We hiked up to the overlook at Pinetop Pass, where we all oohed and aahed at the blue haze that hung over the Great Smoky Mountains to the southwest. Then we headed back down again, with another stop at Hawkins Meadow to wash our sweaty faces in the little brook. It was almost dark when we finally made it back to camp, ate a quick supper in the dining hall, and went to our bunkhouses. Everybody was too tired even for assembly.

"Still no clues," Hallie said glumly, sitting on the foot of her bed. "My locket's still gone."

"Don't worry. I bet there'll be a clue in the morning," Cynthia said confidently.

"How come *you* know so much about this detective stuff, Cynthia?" Mandy asked.

Cynthia colored. "I'm just guessing. Has anybody seen my toothpaste?"

I stared at Cynthia, and something clicked in my mind. She'd found the first clue, and the second one, too.

"Oh, here it is," Cynthia said, locating her toothpaste on the windowsill. She started off down the path in her pajamas toward the bathroom.

"Boy, am I tired," Suzie said, dropping heavily onto her cot. "I don't think I'll *ever* wake up in the morning." She peeked quickly under her cot. It was a habit she'd gotten into since Lilac had made his appearance.

"My feet hurt," Ginger complained.

"Mine, too," I said absently, turning down my blanket. I was thinking about Cynthia and the notes Joan had written on her information card. Cynthia tended to overdramatize things, her mother had reported, and she liked to play jokes on people. Did those jokes include—

My thoughts were interrupted suddenly by a surprised yelp from the direction of the bathroom, and then the sound of feet pounding on the path. The door banged open, and Cynthia dashed in.

"It's a *bear*!" she gasped. "There's a *bear* out there on the path, and he's eating my toothpaste!"

Chapter Eleven

"A bear?" several voices screeched in unison.

"A *big* bear," Cynthia said excitedly, stretching up on tiptoe to measure with her hands over her head. "Taller than me, as tall as a tree!"

I frowned at Cynthia. "Are you sure you're not imagining things?" I asked skeptically. "Did you actually *see* a bear—or did you just think you saw one?"

Cynthia nodded violently. "I *did* see it," she insisted. "It was big and black and—"

"Everything's black in the dark," Ginger pointed out. "Maybe it wasn't a bear at all. Things always look bigger in the dark, too. I bet it was Lilac you saw." She looked at Cynthia sympathetically.

I bit my lip. I was almost a hundred percent sure that this was another one of Cynthia's exaggerations. The best way to deal with the matter was simply to go outside and prove to everybody that there was no bear. I pulled on a sweatshirt and picked up my flashlight.

"Okay," I said nonchalantly. "I'll be right back."

Cynthia stared. "You mean you're actually going out there to *look* for the bear?"

Ah-ha, I thought. She's worried that I'll catch her in her story. "Sure," I said very casually. "I'm not afraid."

Suzie's eyes were as big as oysters. "You're so *brave*, Tabby," she said. She squared her shoulders. "If *you're* brave, so am I. I'll come with you to help."

"Me, too," Hallie said. "Anyway, Ginger's right. It might not be a bear. It's probably just Lilac,"

In the end, all of us went, with me going first, of course, and Cynthia taking up the rear. We crept down the path as quietly as we could. There was a moon, but it didn't help much in the woods. All it did was cast spooky shadows across the path. Behind us, in the center of the camp, somebody must have driven into the clearing. I could hear the sound of car doors slamming and people talking. But in front of us, down the dark path, I heard something else. I shivered.

"Listen, there's an animal down there," Mandy said in a nervous whisper.

"I hear something, too," Linda replied. "But it sounds more like somebody eating ice cream."

I stopped to listen. Definite slurping sounds were coming from the direction of the bathroom. "It's probably just Lilac," I said with a shrug. "He's found something to eat."

"It's a bear, I tell you," Cynthia insisted, but she didn't sound quite as positive as she had a few minutes ago.

We crept closer to the noise. As we came around the curve, I flashed my light up the path. And there, in the middle of the bathroom doorway, was a bear. It was sitting peaceably on its haunches, like a circus bear, squeezing the toothpaste out of the tube it held in its paws. It was slurping it with its big pink tongue the way a person would eat an ice-cream cone. It looked like somebody's pet bear, out for a pleasant evening stroll in the pine forest.

"Oh, my *gosh*," Mandy breathed in an unbelieving tone. "It *is* a bear!"

"I told you," Cynthia said triumphantly.

"But it's not a *wild* bear," I pointed out. "Look, he's wearing a collar. He must be somebody's pet." Suddenly I knew whose pet he was. He was Dean's bear, the cute cub he had mentioned that first evening: Blackstone.

"I don't know," Suzie said, crouching fearfully behind me. "That's kind of a funny-looking collar." It was big and heavy, with some sort of box fastened to it.

"What are we going to do now?" Hallie wanted to know.

"Why," I said confidently, "we're going to capture him. What else?" It would be terrific if I could show Dean that I wasn't such a coward around animals after all. That would really cement our relationship.

Mandy backed up, her eyes wide. "How are we going to do that?" she asked. "Do you really think we should?"

"Sure." I turned to Suzie. "Suzie, do you have any more candy?"

Suzie shuffled her feet a bit. "Well, maybe,"

she said. Reluctantly she reached into her pocket and pulled out a large hunk of peanut brittle. "Will this do?"

"It will if this bear likes peanut brittle," I replied, holding it up. "Here, Blackstone," I said enticingly, still keeping a very safe distance. "Here's some candy for you."

The bear licked the last of the toothpaste from his paw and watched me attentively. Then he sniffed, his little ears pricking forward. He seemed to be in the mood for dessert. I tossed the peanut brittle over his head. The bear dropped Cynthia's empty toothpaste tube, turned on all fours, and shuffled into the bathroom.

I sprang forward and slammed the door behind him. From inside the bathroom came munching sounds, and then, after a minute, the scratch of bear paws on the door.

"Go get Dean," I told Linda. "Tell him we've got his bear." The scratching got louder and more urgent. I got the feeling that the bear wasn't too happy about being shut up in the bathroom.

In a minute Dean came running down the path with a big flashlight. Pete was right behind him, and with Pete were two men I'd never seen before. They wore ranger's uniforms and carried big flashlights also. One of them had a gun.

"Where's the bear?" Dean asked urgently.

"In there," Ginger piped up, pointing toward the bathroom. The bear was thumping on the door now, and beginning to make disgruntled noises. He was clearly out of sorts about the whole business. "Tabby put him in the bathroom," she added proudly. "He really likes peanut brittle."

Dean stared at me. "You did *what*?"

I frowned. I'd thought he'd be pleased that I'd found Blackstone. "It's okay," I told him. "We didn't hurt your bear. Honest. He's eating some of Suzie's candy." There was a crash and the doorframe rattled.

"I guess he's finished the peanut brittle by now," Mandy said. "He wants to come out."

One of the rangers stepped forward. "Did this bear have a collar on?" he asked me.

I nodded.

"Sounds like Bear Number Twenty-seven, for sure," the other ranger said with a grin. He held up his gun and checked something on it. "Is there a window in the place?"

Pete led the rangers around the side of the

bathroom. The girls and I followed at a distance.

"Listen, you're not going to *shoot* the bear, are you?" I asked uneasily. "I mean, he's a pet bear. You can't kill him!"

"It's a tranquilizer gun," Dean explained, turning to me. "They'll put the bear to sleep so they can take him into the woods and turn him loose again." He gave me a curious look. "What's this business about the bear being a pet?"

"Why, it must be Blackstone," I said. "He's wearing a collar."

Dean shook his head as if he couldn't believe what he was hearing. "What that bear is wearing is a *radio* collar, Tabby," he said patiently. "A transmitter. The rangers put it on captured bears to keep track of them. In fact, that's how these guys knew where to come looking for this bear."

"You mean," I said in a wavery voice, "that this is a *wild* bear?"

There was a sharp POP and a loud squeal from inside the bathroom, and then thrashing noises. Soon the thrashing stopped, and there was nothing but silence.

"That's it," one of the rangers said with satisfaction. "Pete, if you and Dean will give us a hand, we can get Number Twenty-seven loaded into the truck."

"I *told* you it was a real bear," Cynthia chortled gleefully. "But you didn't believe me. You all thought I was telling stories."

Dean nodded at Cynthia. "Yeah," he said. "It was a bear, all right." He grinned at me. "For somebody who's a coward about animals," he added, "I'd say you did a great job, Tabby."

"You were so brave, Tabby," Suzie said, in an admiring voice.

I shook my head. "But *Cynthia* is the one who saw the bear first and reported it to the rest of us," I reminded everyone, putting my arm around Cynthia's shoulders. "She's the brave one." Dean gave me a smile. He could tell what I was trying to do.

"Well, then," the ranger said, "maybe this courageous young lady would like something to remember her first bear by." He fished in his pocket and pulled out a gleaming badge. "Cynthia, would you please step forward?"

Cynthia looked at me nervously. "Is it okay?" she whispered.

"Sure," I whispered back, giving her a little push. "You earned it. Go on."

136

The ranger smiled down at her. "Cynthia," he said in an official-sounding voice, "for valor above and beyond duty in reporting the whereabouts of Bear Number Twenty-seven, I hereby designate you an Honorary Smokey Bear Forest Ranger." With a flourish, he leaned forward to pin the badge on her pajamas. Behind us, six girls sighed a collective sigh of admiration. Then Dean began to clap, and everybody else joined in. Cynthia just stood there, scuffing the dirt with her bare toe and looking embarrassed.

The ranger turned. "Let's get that bear loaded," he said. We watched as Pete and Dean and the two rangers loaded the sleeping bear into a sling and carried it down the path to the clearing where the truck was parked. It only took a few minutes to get the bear safely into his cage. With a last thank-you and a wave, the rangers got into the truck and drove off.

"Okay, everybody," I said, "it's time to head back to the cabin."

"Gosh," Cynthia said, looking down at her gleaming badge. "I wonder if I'll be able to sleep tonight." But she and the others turned to go without a word of protest.

Dean took my hand. "I was wondering," he

said, "if you'd like to go for a walk down by the lake. After the girls are asleep, that is."

"Sure," I said with a smile. "That would be great."

"Okay," Dean said. "How about if I meet you by the Assembly Circle in about twenty minutes?"

"I'll be there," I said.

Chapter Twelve

The moon wasn't full, the way it had been the first night; it was a narrow crescent, like a slice of pale silver.

I shivered, and Dean put his arm around me as we sat on the rock. "Cold?" he asked.

"A little," I said, clasping my knees to my chest. But it wasn't the pine-scented breeze that was making me shiver. It was Dean, sitting so close beside me in the moonlight. And *this* time, Mother wasn't anywhere in sight.

His arm tightened. "You know," he said thoughtfully, "that was a good idea you had—praising Cynthia, I mean. You made this evening something she'll always remember and be proud of."

I gave a rueful little laugh. "Well, to tell the truth," I said, "I don't think *any* of us will forget it. I know I won't, anyway. It was quite a shock to find out that the bear wasn't Blackstone."

"I imagine Blackstone is miles away," Dean said, "living peacefully on nuts and berries. But even if he did come back, I wouldn't want to take a chance on getting too close to him. He might remember me, but then again, bears are unpredictable. He might not." He turned to face me. "But I don't want to talk about bears," he said softly.

My heart leapt. "What do you want to talk about?" I whispered.

"About us," he said. His eyes were shadowed, but I could see a faint smile on his lips. "The camp session will be over in a week, you know."

I nodded. "I know," I said sadly. "I wish it didn't have to end."

It was true. A little over a week ago, I'd hated the idea of being sentenced to two whole weeks at Camp Cherokee, and I'd looked forward longingly to spending the last week with Megan at Sail-Away, with its hot showers and television sets and vending machines. But since I'd met Dean, Sail-Away seemed almost like a childish dream, while Camp Cherokee was real and wonderful.

"You know, maybe it doesn't have to end," Dean said slowly. He picked up my hand and held it gently. "At least, not quite so soon, anyway. I'm going to stay on for a week or so to help Pete with some fixups that need to be done around here. I was wondering if maybe you could arrange to stay, too, at least for a few days." He stroked my fingers, not looking at me. "It would give us a little more time to spend together."

I stared at him. Stay at Camp Cherokee with Dean, instead of going to Sail-Away for the last week with Megan? For a moment I thought fleetingly of all the super things I'd be giving up—tennis and volleyball, boiled lobster and stuffed crab, cute guys by the dozens, fast sailboats with polished brass and teak trim. But I wasn't even tempted. I knew what I wanted to do.

"That's a terrific idea, Dean," I said. "I'll ask Pete and Joan in the morning whether they'd mind having an extra guest for a few days."

Dean chuckled. "A guest? I think we should put you to work fixing Lucille's corral. How are you with a hammer?"

141

I laughed, too. "Not as good as I am with a paintbrush," I said happily.

Then we both stopped laughing. The look in Dean's eyes was tender as he touched my cheek with his fingers and turned my head toward him. "Oh, Tabby," he murmured, leaning forward to kiss me. For the next few minutes, I was oblivious to everything around us—the moon, the clouds, the shimmering water—as I lost myself in Dean's arms.

We weren't alone together much longer. But the intruder wasn't Mother. From somewhere behind us in the pine trees there was a querulous *whoo-whoo?* then the swift whoosh of heavy wings, and something landed on my head.

I flinched. For an instant I shut my eyes. And then I opened them again. "It must be Merlin," I said resignedly.

"Yeah," Dean said, taking the owl off my head. "You know, he doesn't just go around landing on *everybody's* head. He must really love you."

I smiled. Dean's eyes were on mine. "Chalk up another great experience," I said. "Being loved by an owl."

"How about just being loved?" Dean asked quietly. He bent to kiss me again.

＊　　＊　　＊

"Hey, Tabby, look!"

I blinked the fog of sleep from my eyes and raised myself up on one elbow. "What is it?" I asked groggily.

Outside the early morning light was a silvery gray, and a soft rain was falling, making a gentle *ssh* among the pine needles. Inside Hallie was bouncing up and down with excitement on the foot of my cot. Please, God, I prayed fervently, don't let it be another wild animal. After last night, I didn't think I could take another animal.

"It's a clue!" Hallie cried. She was holding a little piece of paper. "At least it *looks* like one. But it's got your name on the outside, so we haven't opened it yet."

I blinked again and sat up straight. "A clue?"

Ginger joined Hallie on my cot. "We found it in the bathroom just now," she said importantly.

Cynthia came up to us, struggling to pull her sweatshirt over her head. "Are you going to read it?" she asked in a muffled voice. Her sweatshirt had her Honorary Smokey Bear Forest Ranger badge pinned to it.

"Yes," I told her, taking the piece of paper. On the inside was printed,

If Hallie wants to find her locket,
she should look in her pocket.
When she finds it,
she should look inside it.

I read the little poem aloud as the rest of the girls began to gather around my cot.

"In my *pocket*?" Hallie asked. She patted the pockets of her jeans and scowled. "It's not there. Maybe somebody's playing a trick."

"Don't give up yet," Mandy advised. "Try your *other* pockets."

"Somebody *is* playing a trick!" Hallie wailed after she'd looked in the pockets of everything in her suitcase. "And it's not a very nice one, either."

I bent over the mess of clothes on her cot. "Do you have any other pockets?" I asked. I pointed to the pocket in the side of her suitcase. "What about *that* one?"

Hallie shoved her hand into the pocket and withdrew it. From her fingers dangled something golden and gleaming.

"My locket!" she exclaimed. "We've found it!"

"But you have to look inside it," Linda reminded her. "Remember what the clue said."

Hallie opened the locket. Inside was an-

144

other tiny piece of paper. Hallie unfolded it and read slowly, "P.S. This is the end."

"The end?" Ginger asked with a puzzled frown. "Of what?"

"The end of the game," Cynthia said soberly. "I guess maybe it wasn't such a funny game after all, was it, Tabby?"

"Oh," I said lightly, "it had its moments." I pulled her to me and gave her a big hug, and the Smokey Bear badge scratched my arm. "Listen," I said, "maybe we should have a real scavenger hunt, for the whole camp."

Cynthia looked up, her eyes shining. "You mean it, with real clues and prizes and everything?"

"Right," I said, smiling. "And maybe you'd like to organize it."

"Megan?" I shouted into the phone in Joan's office. "It's Tabby. Can you hear me?"

"Just barely," a tiny voice said. "Where *are* you? On the moon?"

I grinned. She was the same old Megan. "Almost," I shouted. "I'm still at Camp Cherokee. Listen, I'm not coming to Sail-Away for the last week. You'll have to get along without me."

"You're *not*?" Megan sounded startled. "How come? Is your mom making you stay?"

"I'm doing it for love," I said, giggling.

"For love? I thought the oldest guy there was eleven. Isn't that a little young for you?"

"He's one of the counselors. His name is Dean, and he's absolutely perfect." I stopped. "I can't tell you about him over the phone, Megan," I said. "You'll just have to wait until I get back. Or I'll write you a letter, if I can get around to it. How does it feel to be living the luxurious life at Sail-Away? How are the guys?"

There was a pause. "Boring," Megan said finally.

"Boring?" I couldn't believe my ears. "But what about the two great guys you wrote to me about? And the tennis and the sailing and the swimming and—"

"Yes, but I've been doing all that stuff every day for two weeks," Megan said. "I'm getting tired of it. It's almost like being in Washington. What's more, those two great guys turned out to have two great girlfriends back home. The other guys are here mostly to learn how to sail. They're not especially interested in girls." She sighed. "Well, I have to go play another round of volleyball," she said. "See you in a couple of weeks."

"Yeah," I said. "See you." I hung up the phone and turned around. Mother was lounging in the doorway with a huge grin on her face.

"So," she said, "you're going to hang around here for a while, huh?"

"You were listening," I said accusingly.

"From the beginning to the end," Mother admitted. "That's how come I know you're staying. When were you going to get around to telling me?"

"Sooner or later," I said sheepishly. "It's okay if I stay, isn't it?" I added.

Mother nodded. "Sure. But have you figured out yet how you're going to get home?"

"Well, there's always the bus," I said. "Or maybe Dean can bring me. He's got a sister in Washington, and he was thinking of spending a few days with her before school starts." That had been the best news of all, as far as I was concerned. It meant that leaving Camp Cherokee didn't mean saying goodbye to Dean forever.

Mother stepped forward and tugged lightly on my French braid. "It looks as if Camp Cherokee was good for you," she said.

I grinned. "You might say that. We're back on hugging terms now, aren't we?" And when she put her arms around me for the first time in two whole weeks, it felt wonderful.

Wearing high-heeled pumps and a tailored business suit, Cynthia's mother stood beside me as Cynthia loaded her suitcases neatly into the trunk of the car. Then she went to collect her artwork from the display in the crafts cabin. Everybody else had already left, with reluctant goodbyes and promises to write. "It's hard to believe the change that a couple of weeks can make," she said, shaking her head. "Is that really my little girl, doing all those things without being told, and without throwing a temper tantrum?"

I laughed. "Sometimes we do a lot of growing up in a very short time," I said, speaking from experience.

Cynthia came running up and thrust something toward me. "Here," she said. "I want you to have this."

I looked at her gift in surprise. "But it's your very best clay pot," I said. "Don't you want to take it home with you to remind you of all the good times we've had?"

Cynthia shook her head and looked down

proudly at her Camp Cherokee T-shirt, to which her Smokey Bear badge was pinned. "I've got something more important to remind me," she said. Then she suddenly grabbed me around the waist with both arms and held on tight. "I'll miss you, Tabby," she said, her voice muffled.

Dean came up beside us, leading Lucille by her halter. "Leaving, Cynthia?" he asked.

"I wish I didn't have to," Cynthia replied. She looked back at me. "If I write to you, will you write back?"

"Of course I will," I told her.

Cynthia's mother glanced warily at Lucille, then held out her hand to her daughter. "It's time to be going, dear," she said.

Cynthia opened the car door, ignoring her mother's hand. "Listen, Mom," she said excitedly, climbing in, "I've got so much to tell you! See, there was this big, black bear, almost *six* feet high—and he ate my toothpaste and we caught him and put him in the bathroom and the ranger made him go to sleep and then he gave me a badge for being courageous—and we capsized the canoe out in the middle of the lake and everybody had to swim for their lives and Tabby let me organize a scavenger hunt and—"

"Yes, dear," Cynthia's mother replied patiently, going around to the driver's side. She looked over the top of the car at me. "Some things never change," she said in a resigned voice.

"Oh, yes, they do," I told her with a laugh. But I couldn't help feeling a little sorry for Cynthia. Beside me, Dean chuckled, and as they drove off, he slipped his arm around my shoulders and pulled me close.

"I hope you're looking forward to another exciting week at Camp Cherokee," he said, tipping back his hat.

I hugged him tighter. "Actually, I was hoping for a quiet week with you."

"I'm not making any promises," Dean said, laughing.

Behind us, Lucille began to hum.

SWEET DREAMS are fresh, fun and exciting—alive with the flavor of the contemporary teen scene—the joy and doubt of *first love*. If you've missed any SWEET DREAMS titles, then you're missing out on *your* kind of stories, written about people like *you!*

☐ 26976	P.S. I LOVE YOU #1 Barbara P. Conklin	$2.50
☐ 24332	THE POPULARITY PLAN #2 Rosemary Vernon	$2.25
☐ 26613	LITTLE SISTER #5 Yvonne Green	$2.50
☐ 24291	TEN-BOY SUMMER #18 Janet Quin-Harkin	$2.25
☐ 26614	THE POPULARITY SUMMER #20 Rosemary Vernon	$2.50
☐ 27139	101 WAYS TO MEET MR. RIGHT #89 Janet Quin-Harkin	$2.50
☐ 26843	KISS & TELL #92 Janet Quin-Harkin	$2.50
☐ 26743	THE GREAT BOY CHASE #93 Janet Quin-Harkin	$2.50
☐ 27015	FIRST, LAST, AND ALWAYS #96 Barbara P. Conklin	$2.50
☐ 26980	PLAYING FOR KEEPS #104 Janice Stevens	$2.50
☐ 25469	THE PERFECT BOY #105 Elizabeth Reynolds	$2.25
☐ 25470	MISSION: LOVE #106 Kathryn Maris	$2.25
☐ 25535	IF YOU LOVE ME #107 Barbara Steiner	$2.25
☐ 25536	ONE OF THE BOYS #108 Jill Jarnow	$2.25
☐ 25643	NO MORE BOYS #109 Charlotte White	$2.25
☐ 25642	PLAYING GAMES #110 Eileen Hehl	$2.25
☐ 25726	STOLEN KISSES #111 Elizabeth Reynolds	$2.50
☐ 25727	LISTEN TO YOUR HEART #112 Marian Caudell	$2.50
☐ 25814	PRIVATE EYES #113 Julia Winfield	$2.50
☐ 25815	JUST THE WAY YOU ARE #114 Janice Boies	$2.50
☐ 26158	PROMISE ME LOVE #115 Jane Redish	$2.50
☐ 26195	HEARTBREAK HILL #116 Carol MacBain	$2.50
☐ 26196	THE OTHER ME #117 Terri Fields	$2.50

☐ 20293	HEART TO HEART #118 Stefanie Curtis		$2.50
☐ 26339	STAR-CROSSED LOVE #119 Sharon Cadwallader		$2.50
☐ 26340	MR. WONDERFUL #120 Fran Michaels		$2.50
☐ 26418	ONLY MAKE-BELIEVE #121 Julia Winfield		$2.50
☐ 26419	STARS IN HER EYES #122 Dee Daley		$2.50
☐ 26481	LOVE IN THE WINGS #123 Virginia Smiley		$2.50
☐ 26482	MORE THAN FRIENDS #124 Janice Boies		$2.50
☐ 26528	PARADE OF HEARTS #125 Cloverdale Press		$2.50
☐ 26566	HERE'S MY HEART #126 Stefanie Curtis		$2.50
☐ 26567	MY BEST ENEMY #127 Janet Quin-Harkin		$2.50
☐ 26671	ONE BOY AT A TIME #128 Diana Gregory		$2.50
☐ 26672	A VOTE FOR LOVE #129 Terri Fields		$2.50
☐ 26701	DANCE WITH ME #130 Jahnna Beecham		$2.50
☐ 26865	HAND-ME-DOWN HEART #131 Mary Schultz		$2.50
☐ 26790	WINNER TAKES ALL #132 Laurie Lykken		$2.50
☐ 26864	PLAYING THE FIELD #133 Eileen Hehl		$2.50
☐ 26789	PAST PERFECT #134 Fran Michaels		$2.50
☐ 26902	GEARED FOR ROMANCE #135 Shan Finney		$2.50
☐ 26903	STAND BY FOR LOVE #136	Carol MacBain	$2.50
☐ 26948	ROCKY ROMANCE #137 Sharon Dennis Wyeth		$2.50
☐ 26949	HEART & SOUL #138	Janice Boies	$2.50
☐ 27005	THE RIGHT COMBINATION #139 Jahnna Beecham		$2.50
☐ 27061	LOVE DETOUR #140	Stefanie Curtis	$2.50
☐ 27062	WINTER DREAMS #141	Barbara Conklin	$2.50

Prices and availability subject to change without notice.

- -

Bantam Books, Dept. SD, 414 East Golf Road, Des Plaines, IL 60016

Please send me the books I have checked above. I am enclosing $_____
(please add $2.00 to cover postage and handling). Send check or money order
—no cash or C.O.D.s please.

Mr/Ms _____

Address_____

City/State _____ Zip _____

SD—5/88

Please allow four to six weeks for delivery. This offer expires 11/88.

BANTAM
SHOP-AT-HOME
C·A·T·A·L·O·G

Special Offer
Buy a Bantam Book
for only 50¢.

Now you can order the exciting books you've been wanting to read straight from Bantam's latest catalog of hundreds of titles. *And* this special offer gives you the opportunity to purchase a Bantam book for only 50¢. Here's how:

By ordering any five books at the regular price per order, you can also choose any other single book listed (up to a $5.95 value) for only 50¢. Some restrictions do apply, so for further details send for Bantam's catalog of titles today.

Just send us your name and address and we'll send you Bantam Book's SHOP AT HOME CATALOG!